"No."

"Jon, please. It's only for one night. It'll be fun."

Jon Stuart listened to the reproachful voice on the telephone, gazed disbelievingly at the ceiling, and said, "No. It will not be fun because I'm not going to do it."

"I thought we were friends...."

"Stop wheedling. The answer's no." He hung up on her indignant response in which the word *patronizing* figured prominently.

"What was *that* all about?" his partner asked.

"Well, don't quote me," Jon drawled, "but I think I've just turned down the opportunity to become engaged to the most attractive blond dingbat you've ever seen. Jessica Delaney."

Kay Gregory grew up in England, but moved to Canada as a teenager. She now lives in Vancouver with her husband, two sons, one dog and two ferrets. She has had innumerable jobs, some interesting, some extremely boring, which have often provided background for her books. Now that she is writing Harlequin romance novels, Kay thinks she has at last found a job that she won't find necessary to change.

GOODBYE
DELANEY
Kay Gregory

Harlequin Books

TORONTO • NEW YORK • LONDON
AMSTERDAM • PARIS • SYDNEY • HAMBURG
STOCKHOLM • ATHENS • TOKYO • MILAN
MADRID • WARSAW • BUDAPEST • AUCKLAND

To: Deiter & Elvira Warmbold
Who showed me a new and different Thunder Bay

Original hardcover edition published in 1991
by Mills & Boon Limited

ISBN 0-373-17135-8

Harlequin Romance first edition May 1993

GOODBYE DELANEY

CHAPTER ONE

JON swore under his breath as the phone on his desk buzzed for the sixth time in fifteen minutes, but, automatically, and without taking his eyes from the stack of printouts in front of him, he reached out an arm for the receiver. Then he listened for a moment to the soft, feminine voice murmuring at him over the wires, gazed disbelievingly at the ceiling, and said, "No."

"Oh, Jon. You don't mean that." The voice quivered with injured reproach.

Steady gray eyes returned resolutely to the printouts. "Cut it out, Delaney. I've known you too long for your playacting to work on me."

He heard a light, very infectious giggle. "I know you have. I was only six when Roger brought you home from school that first time, wasn't I? And I tried to tell you I wasn't really his sister."

Jon sighed. "If I remember, you said you were the orphaned daughter of an Indian chief who had been drowned heroically while trying to rescue your mother— a princess of course—as she was tumbling briskly over the edge of Niagara Falls."

"That's right. And you didn't believe me."

Jon gave up trying to carry on with his work, stretched long legs comfortably in front of him, and leaned back in his executive chair. "No, I did not believe you. Indian chiefs' daughters don't usually have curly blond ringlets. Now, my dear, charming as these reminiscences are, I have work to do, so if you'll excuse me..."

"Jon!" All his caller's considerable dramatic projection was poured into the way she wailed his name, and in spite of himself Jon found that he was smiling.

"What?" he asked resignedly.

"Jon, please. It's only for one night. It'll be fun."

"It will not be fun because I'm not going to do it. And, in any case, what would you do if someone at that party knew me?"

"Oh, that won't happen. It's only for staff, and you don't know anyone who works at Whitefish Lodge. Do you?"

"No." He was still smiling, but with rather less patience than before.

"Then you'll do it?"

"No!" The smile disappeared completely as he leaned forward over the desk and roared into the receiver. "No, Delaney, I am not falling in with another of your crazy schemes. Forget it."

"I thought we were friends..."

"Stop wheedling. The answer's 'no.'"

When the soft voice started to tell him how desperately she needed him, and how he was the only one she could possibly ask for help, he interrupted again.

"Delaney."

"Yes, Jon?"

"I told you to forget it. Now be a good girl for once, and *do* what you're told!"

When she responded with an indignant stream of abuse in which the word "patronizing" figured prominently, he repeated that he had work to do, if she didn't mind, and hung up the phone in her ear.

"What was *that* all about?" asked his partner, Brad, who had wandered into the office in time to hear the receiver crash loudly back onto its cradle.

Jon sighed, picked up a pen, and tapped it thoughtfully against the edge of his desk. "Well, don't quote me," he drawled, "but if I'm not mistaken I think I've just turned down the opportunity to become engaged to an unusually attractive blond dingbat with the most striking indigo eyes you've ever seen."

Brad eyed his friend warily. "And what, may I ask, do you mean by that incomparable expression?" he inquired, raising a pair of nicely arched eyebrows.

"Dingbat? In this case a combination of ding-a-ling and batty, I should think—an irrepressibly engaging nut case. In other words, Jessica Delaney."

"Ah," said Brad, "I begin to see... All the same, old friend, are you *sure* you haven't been indulging in too much sun?"

Jon shook his head, and pointed out that it happened to be September, and there hadn't been any sun for a week.

Several miles away, on the other side of Thunder Bay in a green and brown family house not far from Centennial Park, the dingbat in question hung up the phone with a bang, and said, "Damn. The rat won't do it."

"What rat?" A fair, freckle-faced teenager, just home from school, pulled his nose from a car magazine as his sister, indigo eyes flashing, stormed noisily into the living room and flung herself into a chair.

"Jon Stuart."

"Oh. Some rat." He spoke with the wistful young man's envy of shoulders, girth and muscles he had yet to attain for himself.

"Mm." His sister's big eyes deepened, as she continued regretfully, "He would have been a perfect fiancé. You know, dark blond hair, nice gray eyes, endlessly long legs—and he's even a chartered accountant."

Her brother stared at her, and then looked hopefully in the direction of the door. "Jessica Delaney, have you gone stark, raving mad?" He started to get up from a beige-colored armchair on which his jeans had left a thin layer of grease.

"Oh, Nick. Of course I haven't. I only wanted him to be my fiancé for one night."

"Why?" Nick sat down again, intrigued despite his better judgment, and as he did so Jessica sprang up restlessly and stalked across to the window.

"Well," she began, not looking at him, "when I gave up teaching because I wanted to write a book I thought I'd just stay home and get on with it. But I'm finding I miss the contact with other people—not to mention the money——"

"Right. So you applied for that receptionist's job down the highway, at Whitefish Lodge Motor Hotel. You don't need a fiancé for that, Jess."

"But that's just it. I do." Jessica swung around to face him. "Actually I need a husband, but as I don't keep spare husbands tucked away in drawers for rainy days I told Mr. Sanegra, the owner, that I was getting married soon. Then I told him we weren't going on a honeymoon because my intended was a sober chartered accountant, and we wanted to save money. I didn't think he'd like it if he thought I might ask for time off right away..."

"Jess, what the hell are you talking about? Why should you need a husband?" Nick tossed his magazine on the floor and leaned toward her. As she laughed ruefully and threw herself back in her chair, he added with a brotherly grin, "If all ex-teachers are as crazy as you are it's no wonder our schools are so mixed up."

"You sound just like Dad. I'm not crazy, and, as you very well know, I did an excellent job with the kids. Little ones always seem to like me." Jessica put her nose in the air and looked pious.

"All right, so they do. It figures. They think you're one of them. But if you don't explain what you're talking about, Jess, I think *I'm* going to go nuts."

"You haven't given me a chance yet," she complained. When Nick responded with a loud snort, she insisted crossly, "Well, you haven't. The thing is, when I got out to Whitefish this morning my friend, Brenda, cornered me outside and told me I probably wouldn't get the job after all because Mr. Sanegra has a thing about single women. Brenda's the receptionist who's leaving to have a baby——"

"I know," said Nick impatiently. "You already told me."

"Yes, of course I did, but as cars are usually the only things that hold your attention for more than two minutes I thought you might have forgotten," replied Jessica with sisterly forthrightness. "Anyway, Brenda said Mr. Sanegra has decided he wants a married woman for the job. Apparently, before he hired her he had a string of desk clerks who kept showing up late with red eyes in purple bags after wild nights out with their boyfriends. And his wife gave him hell every time because the Sanegras live in a suite at the Lodge and she always got stuck to answer the phone and check out guests in the mornings——"

"Tough," interrupted Nick. "He can't refuse to hire you on those grounds, Jess. Discrimination on the basis of marital status is against the Ontario Human Rights Code."

Nick had acquired several speeding tickets over the past year, and had recently developed a keen interest in matters legal.

"Huh." Jessica gave a scornful little laugh. "You know as well as I do he'd find a way to get around that one. He'd just say some other applicant is better suited."

"Yeah, I guess so. All the same, Jess, I don't see why inventing a fiancé helps much."

"It didn't." Jessica sighed, and ran a hand distractedly through her hair. "I don't even know why I did it. Of course it got me the job all right, but, when he asked me to bring my 'young man' to a farewell party he and his wife are giving for Brenda this evening, instead of making an intelligent excuse...I accepted."

Nick shook his head. "And you tell me *I'm* crazy because I spend all the money I make from my job at the snack bar on cars that sometimes don't work!" He picked up his magazine, and slouched across to the door. When he reached it he paused, scratched his head, and added, "I don't get it. You're not really bananas, and Jon Stuart's not an easy man to fool. Matter of fact I was always sort of glad he wasn't around much by the time I was old enough to get into trouble."

Jessica eyed him gloomily. "I know. He can be an awful spoilsport when he doesn't approve of you. He often used not to approve of me," she added wistfully.

"That's what Roger said. And Mom. Though they both thought he put up with more than he should've done. But I still don't see what in hell made you think he was likely to go for this latest brainwave of yours."

"Well," said Jessica reflectively, "he wasn't *always* a spoilsport. Really, most of the time he was nice. Sometimes I'd catch him looking at me, and I just knew he was trying not to laugh. And other times he'd shake his head and tell me to go ahead—like the day he caught me using all the flour in the house to bake Mom and Dad a rock-hard, three-tiered cake with purple icing. I'd also decorated every room in the house with toilet paper streamers and soaped 'Happy Anniversary' all over the windows. He didn't stop me doing that, but afterward he made me clean up the mess—and I think *he* replaced the flour and toilet paper."

"Yeah," said Nick. "I heard about that. And I heard about the time he just about scalped you when you pretended you'd fallen out of the window on April Fool's Day, and scared Mom and Dad half to death."

"He did. He wasn't too nice when he caught me halfway up the telephone pole, either."

"Mm." Nick grinned. "I think I've got it. If it won't hurt anyone Jon's capable of aiding and abetting. If it will he'll come down on you like a ton of bricks."

Jessica nodded. "That's about the size of it. But he won't aid and abet me this time. The rat. And I really don't see why not."

Nick stopped grinning, and looked pompous. "I should hope not. He's a respectable chartered accountant." He pulled his face into a reasonable impersonation of a magistrate about to pass judgment.

"You had to say that, didn't you?" said Jessica, picking up the nearest cushion.

"Of course," he agreed, ducking automatically as she threw it. "But good luck anyway, big sister. You'll need it. Perhaps you can arrange to crash your car on the way to the party, or come down with the chicken pox or something."

Jessica shuddered as he slammed the door behind him and disappeared, whistling unconcernedly.

All very well for him, she reflected glumly, but *he* doesn't happen to want that job.

Besides, she'd already thought of car crashes and chicken pox, and neither of them seemed calculated to inspire confidence in a new employer who stressed the importance of responsibility, reliability and good health.

You've done it again, Jessica, she told herself disgustedly—and just when you were so certain you'd outgrown that childhood passion for story telling, and channeled it safely into your new career as a writer. She sighed. Apparently old habits died hard.

For a moment she sat still, glaring into space, then she jumped up and returned to the window. The September sunlight glinted off her shining hair, creating a halo effect—that she knew she didn't deserve—in the mirror over the mantel. Thank heaven her parents were celebrating her father's retirement from the bank with a trip to Europe. They'd have a fit if they found out about this idiotic mess she'd got into. Jessica rolled her eyes up, shuddering, then remembered that if her mother and father had been at home she wouldn't be here to see to Nick in the first place. She'd be back in her own apartment writing her mystery novel.

She watched a solitary red-winged blackbird glide gently down out of the clouds to alight on the small maple tree growing at the bottom of the garden. But her mind wouldn't concentrate on bird life. Instead it returned like a boomerang to Jon and her current predicament.

It hadn't been until she was driving home from her successful interview with Mr. Sanegra that she had thought of a way out of the glue she had got herself into. A way out with dark blond hair who really *was* a chartered accountant called John—without an "H," though—as well as being her married brother's old school friend. Jon Stuart, who had no brothers or sisters of his own, had spent most of his teenage years hanging around the Delaney house teasing his friend's little sister, listening to her stories, encouraging her undoubted talent for drama, and generally being a much more brotherly big brother than Roger had ever been. Good old easygoing Jon, who could always be counted on in a crisis, and had shouldered the blame for so many of her childhood escapades.

Good old Jon, who in this latest hour of her need was unaccountably refusing to "play ball."

Jessica stared at the tall trees bordering the park. They were just beginning to turn color. Just as Jon had suddenly turned. Why? It couldn't be because of Carol, his most recent girlfriend, because Carol was singing in Winnipeg this month.

She pulled moodily at a button on her pink-checked shirt. It *would* have been fun to take him to the party this evening and pretend he was her fiancé. She had always enjoyed playacting, as he had rudely pointed out, and, next to the story telling which had got her into so much trouble in the past, her dramatic ability had been one of her chief claims to fame at school. Really, he wasn't being at all obliging. Her little deception would hurt nobody. As Nick said, Jon had always drawn the line at that. But it *would* be amusing, if he would only cooperate, and in a week or so she could tell Mr. Sanegra the wedding was off. By that time she would have proved her reliability.

Reluctantly, Jessica found herself smiling at her own rationalizations. Nick was right. She *was* crazy. Twenty-six-year-old ex-schoolteachers didn't invent wildly improbable stories about nonexistent fiancés just to get jobs they could manage quite well without. Nor did they lure respectable chartered accountants into taking part in a fraud...

At that point in her musings Jessica frowned, because it was just beginning to dawn on her that what was aggravating her more than anything else was not that she would now have to find a suitable excuse to give to Mr. Sanegra for her lack of a partner, but that Jon Stuart, that pillar of reliable support, was not falling into line with her wishes as he always had. Well, *almost* always.

It was an unexpected and unwelcome shock, *and*— she was unwillingly forced to admit—as usual Jon had right on his side.

Which only increased her irritation, and did not make his refusal in any way easier to take.

It was after five, and she was beginning to prepare supper for herself and her brother when Nick stuck his head around the kitchen door and asked, as though he'd had a flash of inspiration, "Hey, Jess? You know when you said your fiancé was a chartered accountant, and then didn't have the sense to make up an excuse about the party? Was that because you really *would* like to marry Jon?"

Jessica dropped a tomato-stained spatula onto the floor, and spots which looked like blood spattered in every direction. "No," she said emphatically as she bent to retrieve it. "It most certainly was not. I can't think of anyone I'd less like to marry than that man. He's a smug, patronizing old *bore*."

Nick's blue eyes widened, and there was a sudden stillness in the air as she finished speaking, but before she could turn around a deep voice drawled softly through the open window, "Thanks very much, Delaney. They always say listeners hear no good of themselves, don't they? Now I know why."

Jessica dropped the spatula again, picked it up in a hand that shook slightly and, when she finally turned to the window, found herself looking up into a big, bronzed, very masculine face with a line of faded scar tissue across the forehead—and her gaze was immediately riveted by the flat, calm stare of a man's gray eyes. One large hand was resting on the window frame above

her severely. But his eyes rested on her with a warmth she found disconcerting.

"I'm not incompetent." She tossed her head. "I can make spaghetti and chilli and omelets——"

"When she's not throwing them on the floor," interrupted Nick from his corner. "She's pretty good at ordering Chinese and Kentucky Fried and pizza, as well. *Are* you staying for supper, Jon? You'll be taking your life in your hands."

Jessica threw a tea towel at him, and Jon replied with just a trace of censure, "Yes, I'll stay. I'm sure your sister won't expect me to eat it off the floor. And before you get *too* carried away by your own wit, young man, I suggest you take a turn at cooking for yourself. It's a creative art that doesn't come naturally to everyone, and I'm willing to bet Jessica has been doing all the kitchen duty since your parents left. Hasn't she?"

Nick grinned sheepishly, and grunted something which sounded like an affirmative before ducking through the door with unusual haste and disappearing beneath the bright orange Cyclone Spoiler which took up most of the driveway.

Jessica, who had been looking for a second tea towel to throw at Jon on general principles, changed her mind and laughed instead.

"You sure got rid of him in a hurry." She chuckled, and began to run a damp mop over the red-tiled floor.

"That was the general idea. I wanted to talk to you."

When Jessica put the mop back in the corner and turned around, startled, she saw that Jon was efficiently mixing up tomato sauce and sliding thin tubes of pasta into water that was already boiling briskly.

She opened her mouth to speak, then closed it again, because she had just discovered that Jon Stuart from the rear was a remarkably appealing proposition. Her eyes ran over the muscles moving beneath his sweatshirt, and then dropped almost guiltily to the dark pants fitting snugly over his thighs. Mmm. Very nice. And to think she'd never really noticed this delectable vision that had been under her nose for so long.

Well, not always under her nose, she corrected herself. For the past three years or so she hadn't seen much of Jon. At one time he had been at the house almost every day, and there was that one summer—when he had been between girlfriends and apparently in no hurry to acquire another—that she and Jon, and Roger and his future wife had spent a lot of time together, swimming, playing tennis and hiking in the Northern Ontario forests. Then Roger had married and moved to Toronto.

Jon had come over only once after that, and they had gone swimming at Boulevard Lake. Just the two of them. She must have been about twenty-two at the time. She remembered that she had teasingly stolen his towel and run off with it. He had chased her, and when he'd caught up with her she had tripped and grabbed his arm so that both of them collapsed onto the grass at the edge of the water. For a moment his body had covered hers, pressing her into the ground as he laughed down at her. Then his gray eyes had seemed to darken with some startled emotion she didn't quite understand. And then she did understand. As he'd lain there, not moving, with his warm breath brushing her cheek, she had become aware that she had seen just that look in the eyes of some of the young men she had gone out with. Put simply, it was lust. Or, more politely, desire. Only this was Jon...

"Hey," she had cried, flushing with indignant embarrassment. "It's me—Delaney. Your old friend's little sister. Remember?"

Jon had sworn fluently under his breath, and pushed himself away from her with an abruptness that left her gasping. The next instant he was hauling her on to her feet and telling her to stop behaving like a silly child. His tone and his words were far more severe and censorious than her lighthearted theft had deserved, and she'd sensed that something had happened in those few seconds which would subtly change their relationship—in spite of the fact that for an uncomfortable moment there she had almost expected to find herself over his knee, just as if she were the silly child he had called her.

It had been a subdued and silent pair who'd made their way home that afternoon, and very shortly after that Jon had met a new girlfriend. There had been a number of girlfriends since then, none of them lasting very long, and for the past few months he had been going out with Carol, a local girl who had made good singing on the night-club circuit. Some months after the incident by the lake Jessica had started going out with Richard. Once in a while she had continued to run into Jon, of course, when he happened to drop in on her parents, and he was as friendly and affectionate as ever. But there was a certain constraint about him that hadn't been there before, as well as a careful avoidance of any subject that wasn't entirely impersonal. She had resented his reserve in a way, having dismissed that brief incident as nothing more than an aberration brought on by their unheard-of proximity. But in truth she hadn't thought much about him for months.

Staring at his back now, admiring the easy way he moved, she wondered if he ever thought of that day... Funny, this was the first time it had actually occurred to her that she might have missed an opportunity. And how she could possibly have failed to observe.... But perhaps she had been too absorbed with Richard. More fool her.

At this point Jon gave up waiting for Jessica to answer him, and swung around to see what was causing her uncharacteristic silence. He was just in time to catch her moistening her lips.

Raising heavy eyebrows that were darker than his hair, he smiled quizzically as her face turned a bright, fire-engine red.

"Like what you see?" he inquired lazily. "I'm beginning to feel less of a senile old bore by the minute."

"Oh, shut up," said Jessica, her color fading immediately as she found herself trying not to laugh. "What do you want to talk to me about then, Mr. Know-It-All?"

"Our engagement," he replied, turning back to the stove and beginning to stir vigorously at the sauce.

Jessica saw that his sleeves were pushed up to his elbows, and she observed the bronzed forearms with a startling flick of... Oh. Oh, dear. No, she couldn't possibly be feeling what she thought she was feeling. This was Jon, after all. She pushed the thought away firmly. Then she took in his words, gasped, and said quickly, "What? What engagement?"

"You proposed to me this afternoon. Remember?"

"Oh, *that* engagement." The breath she had been holding came out in a rush, and she moved toward him, making a halfhearted attempt to grab the spoon he was wielding.

He maintained his grip on it, and said smoothly, "Yes, that engagement. Did you have another one in mind?"

"No, of course not. Don't be silly. And why are you cooking the supper?"

"Because Nick's brotherly warnings, my own memory of your past culinary efforts, and the condition of your kitchen floor all lead me to believe I stand a better chance of eating if I see to it myself.'' He pulled the spaghetti off the stove, and emptied it smartly into a colander.

Jessica stared morosely at his back. "If you think I'm such a klutz, why did you stay, then? And chartered accountants aren't supposed to cook.''

"Good Lord, aren't they?" He looked up in feigned horror. "If only I'd known..."

"Oh, shut up," said Jessica for the second time.

"No."

"What do you mean, no?"

"Just that. I want to talk to you, and I have no intention of shutting up."

"Oh." Jessica decided she'd said enough, and waited for him to go on.

"That's better," said Jon, when he saw her unusual eyes fixed on him expectantly. "Now *you* shut up for a minute, Delaney, at least long enough for me to tell you that I've changed my mind. Or don't chartered accountants change their minds either?"

Jessica frowned. "I guess they do, if you say so. What have you changed yours about, then?"

He gave the sauce one last, determined stir, and dumped the spaghetti back into the pan. "About tonight, Delaney. I've decided to be your fiancé, after all."

"You have? Oh, Jon, you angel.'' Without thinking, Jessica reacted as she always had to this big lion of a man, who was now reaching up to rummage in her cupboards for plates. She flung her arms around his waist and hugged him.

For a moment Jon froze, and then he turned very slowly within the circle of her arms to drop his own long arms gently over her shoulders. An endless time seemed to pass as he stared down at the long face with the wide mouth, straight nose and startled eyes framed in dark lashes.

Jessica was aware that by all conventional standards she ought to have been considered ugly. But she had also been told, by Richard and other young men, that her unusual features were thrown together in a combination that was strangely attractive. Now, as it became disconcertingly obvious that her closeness was having a very physical effect on Jon, she knew that her tall, almost angular body wasn't unattractive either—and with an embarrassed little laugh she pulled away.

"Sorry," she muttered. "I wasn't thinking."

"Do you ever?" His voice was unusually gruff—and he was raising his eyebrows in that irritating way again.

"Oh, shut..." She stopped abruptly, found the plates he had been searching for, and thumped them onto the kitchen table. "What made you change your mind, Jon?"

"Well," he replied, smiling that long, lazy smile that she'd never before realized was so maddeningly appealing, "after I hung up the phone——"

"In my ear."

"In your ear, it occurred to me that I'd never had the opportunity to be engaged to my favorite dingbat before. As it happens I have nothing much to do this evening— and besides, you're right. It may be fun."

Jessica eyed him doubtfully. "You don't sound nearly as stuffy and chartered as you did on the phone. Am I really your favorite dingbat?"

He grinned. "Definitely. But I wish you wouldn't accuse me of being chartered."

"But you are," said Jessica, with irrefutable logic. "It's what you do."

"And that makes me stuffy?" There was a cool, reserved note in his voice.

She shrugged. "Oh, I don't know. You are sometimes, you know. But you're still my favorite honorary
brother."

"Hmm. So the dingbat and her honorary brother will
eat cold spaghetti together, and then adjourn to the festivities at Whitefish. It promises to be a riotous evening."
His voice still held that cool, flat note.

"Oh, it won't be so bad," said Jessica quickly, "and
I'm sure the spaghetti's still warm. I'll see if I can fish
Nick out from under his car, then, shall I?"

Without looking at him again she hurried outside,
partly to urge her greasy young brother to emerge from
beneath his mechanical haven, but mostly to get away
from Jon. She frowned, kicking thoughtfully at the
gravel in the driveway. Except for that once, Jon had
never made her feel uncomfortable before. Guilty,
perhaps, but not truly uncomfortable—as she was now.
She supposed it was because he seemed different today.
Oh, sure, he was still his old, teasing self, but there was
something else there now as well. Something withdrawn
and a little judgmental. And it unnerved her.

Irritably she called to Nick to hurry up and get himself
washed for supper.

The spaghetti, which as Jon had predicted was definitely past its prime, was consumed with dedication and
very little conversation. In Nick's case this was because
he was anxious to retreat to his beloved car. In Jessica's,
her silence was caused mainly by belated qualms about
the "riotous" evening ahead of her with this strangely
unpredictable Jon. What had she got herself—and him—
into? To add to her confusion he looked entirely un-
concerned about it, although he didn't seem inclined to
talk much.

As soon as they had finished Nick slammed the door
shut with explosive force, jumped into his Cyclone, and

roared away down the street. Jon's eyes followed him, as he rose without haste to help Jessica clear away the dishes.

"Doesn't that young man ever stay to give you a hand?" he asked.

"When he thinks of it," replied Jessica, pulling a face, "but most of the time he only thinks about cars. He's just sold his Volkswagen, which went beautifully, in order to make enough money to keep his Cyclone, which rarely goes, not going."

Jon choked into the coffee he was finishing. "No wonder you're a nut case, Delaney," he muttered. "It must be genetic."

Jessica eyed him sourly. "If you think I'm such an idiot, Jon Stuart, I don't see why you're coming with me this evening."

"Precisely because you are an idiot, of course."

"I thought you said you'd decided it might be fun."

"I lied. I see little prospect of fun in an evening spent pretending to be something I'm not in order to keep my old friend's crazy sister out of trouble."

Jessica glowered silently. She was not at a loss for words by any means, but she was afraid that if she responded to his caustic comments in kind she might jeopardize her chances of luring him to the party. So she bit her lip, put her nose in the air, and stalked into her bedroom to change.

Half an hour later, wearing a soft mauve dress and an amethyst necklace that matched her eyes, she stalked out to the road and sank regally onto the passenger seat of Jon's New Yorker. At least, she would have sunk regally if she hadn't tripped over his leather-shod foot and landed in an ungainly heap on the floor.

"You did that on purpose, didn't you?" she accused, as they pulled away from the curb.

"Did I?" Gray eyes glinted sideways at her, and the side of his mouth which she could see twisted slightly.

Jessica tightened her lips. There was no sense trying to get the better of Jon in this mood. He would only laugh at her.

They sped along the highway without speaking, Jon's strong hands resting lightly on the wheel. Jessica forced her eyes to look past him to the green and gold foliage lining the road. Soon this route she would be traveling every morning would blaze with the colors of autumn. But it would be dark, and she wouldn't see the flaming maples or the deep gold sheen of birches, poplars and alders.

She sighed, and glanced back at Jon. The window was open, and his heavy blond hair waved enticingly against his neck in the dusk.

"What's the matter, Delaney?" he asked softly.

"Nothing."

"Hmm." He shifted his hand on the wheel. "Tell me something..."

"What?"

"How come I'm the lucky candidate for this mad charade? Is it because Richard had the brains to refuse?"

"I'm not seeing Richard any more." She stared straight ahead through the window.

"Ah. Well, his successor, then."

"There isn't a successor."

"You surprise me."

"Why?"

His lip curled cynically. "Because, knowing you as I do, I shouldn't have thought you'd be one to let the grass grow under your feet. I'd have expected you to be on the prowl for a replacement once Richard was out of the picture."

Jessica's hands twisted in her lap, and she dug her nails hard into her palms. A replacement for Richard? Dear God, that still hurt. She shifted restlessly against the leather seat, remembering that there had been a time, once, when Richard had been the center of her world. Even after the first heartrending betrayal she had continued to love him with a loyalty born of grief and desperation. But over the months he had chipped away at that love until finally there was nothing left but emptiness and despair. So she had ended it, covering her desolation with careless laughter and the flippant declaration that she didn't need a man in her life. But in truth she was afraid to give her heart again. It hurt too much. And now Jon was talking to her about replacements. Jon, whom she had called on for help because he was "safe."

"Thanks," she said, not looking at him. "So now I'm a predatory female, am I, as well as a nut case?" Her voice dropped to a low, unconsciously wistful cadence. "Well, I can tell you one thing, Jon. A year going out with Richard is enough to cure anyone of prowling." Without thinking, she added, "Obviously you've never tried it."

"I should hope not."

Jessica, noting the amused curl to his lips, and still torn by her bitter memories, felt something snap. "Oh!" she cried. "Oh! You are the most unfeeling, irritating, infuriating——"

"Hold it," he interrupted. "Keep that up, Delaney, and I shall turn this car smartly around and take you straight home to bed."

"Like hell you will."

"In a purely paternal sense," he said dryly. "As in, 'if you don't behave yourself, young lady, you'll be sent to bed.'"

"Unfeeling *and* patronizing," Jessica shot back. "Anyway, you can't take me home. Mr. Sanegra expects me—us."

"Then behave yourself."

Jessica glared at him. "Why *did* you agree to come, Jon? It's obvious you don't want to."

"No, I don't. Calculated lunacy is not my style. But I was afraid if I didn't keep an eye on you you'd talk some thoroughly unsuitable creep into playing your little game, and end up making an even bigger fool of yourself than usual. And it seemed to me that this job must be pretty important to you or you wouldn't have come up with such a crazy scheme in the first place."

She was about to reply acidly that apparently he was under the impression that she was incapable of doing anything that *wasn't* crazy, when it occurred to her that he was probably telling her the stark truth. It would be just like him to decide she needed a chaperon. She was twenty-six years old and had taught in a school for four years, but to him she was probably still just Roger's naughty little sister. The one he had spoiled and protected for twenty years. To be fair, though, what he called "this mad charade" couldn't be expected to change his opinion of her mental age and, also to be fair, he undoubtedly did want to help her keep her job, if only because *she* wanted it. Keeping little Jessica happy and laughing had become a casual habit with him. Except, of course, when she ran up against that indefinable barrier beyond which it was impossible to shift him.

Then, when he decided to hold his ground, Jon Stuart was as immovable as a rock.

She looked at his steady hands on the wheel as he swung the car round a corner, and said reluctantly, "Yes, the job is quite important to me. At least, not the job itself so much, but it's just what I need at the moment because—well, because it will leave me lots of time to write my book.''

"Mm.'' He grunted, and then added curiously, ''If you were going to take a job anyway, Delaney, why in the world did you ever give up teaching?''

''I told you. To write my mystery.'' There was an undertone of defensiveness in her reply, because she half expected him to laugh. ''Don't you understand that I'll never be satisfied until I've proved I can at least get it finished?''

''Mm.'' He grunted again. ''But why not keep on teaching, and finish the book in the evenings? And if time is the problem why bother working at Whitefish? You're not making sense, Delaney. Though why that should surprise me, I don't know.''

''I *am* making sense. Don't be so superior. You see, there was always so much work to do at night while I was teaching, and then when the holidays came the sun was shining, the water was warm, the tennis courts were waiting—and my apartment's not very big...''

''I get the picture. In other words, your good intentions evaporated at the first sign of warm weather, and the mystery never did get written. Typical.''

''It is *not* typical. Stop patronizing me, Jon. Can't you understand that what I need now is a nine-to-five—or in this case seven-to-three—job that will give me plenty of time to write in the evenings? I miss the kids and being with other people. I also miss the money, and Whitefish is the answer to a prayer. Pleasant, scenic surroundings near the lake, not much pressure and, above all, lots of time to write.''

''All right. Point taken. How's the book coming along?''

Jessica glanced at him suspiciously, wondering if he was patronizing her again. But his features were perfectly straight, and when he turned his head to smile at her she recognized a familiar friendly interest in her doings.

It was all she needed.

For the remainder of the journey to Whitefish Jon was treated to an enthusiastic account of the blood-stained tennis ball in Chapter Two, leading to the discovery of a decapitated tea taster in Chapter Three, and the violent encounter between the Reverend Michael McGillicuddy and Colonel McWhirter of the Guards in Chapter Four.

By the time they reached their destination his eyes were glazing over, and Jessica stopped abruptly.

"You're bored, aren't you?" she accused.

"No. Fascinated. You have a fiendish imagination, Delaney. Remind me never to inspire your more homicidal inclinations, won't you?"

Jessica laughed. "You're always inspiring them," she retorted.

But both of them knew she didn't mean it.

The party was in full swing when they arrived. Brenda and her husband, Ben, the guests of honor, had already consumed too much punch—probably, Jessica thought, in order to deaden the embarrassment of having to listen to the over-effusive speech Mr. Sanegra was making about the anticipated arrival of their first baby.

She grabbed Jon by the arm, and tried to drag him unobtrusively behind a high-backed chair that was as flowery and overstuffed as the speech, but unfortunately there was nothing remotely unobtrusive about six feet four of heroically built chartered accountant.

Mr. Sanegra stopped in mid-effusion, beamed, and said loudly, "Ah, Jessica, my dear. And your husband-to-be. Delighted you were able to make it."

About a dozen pairs of eyes glanced at them curiously, but the pair belonging to Brenda widened in amazement, and when Jessica saw her open her mouth she realized that at any moment her friend was going to spill the beans. "Yes, this is Jon, Mr. Sanegra," she said hastily. "Er—we're—er—going to be married soon."

Brenda's mouth closed with a startled snap, and Mr. Sanegra's bushy eyebrows rose into his steel gray brush-cut. "Yes, so you have already told me, my dear," he murmured, obviously puzzled.

Jessica swallowed. "Oh. Yes, of course I did. But please don't let us interrupt you, Mr. Sanegra."

From the corner of her eye she saw Brenda indicate with a frown that she would be more than happy to see the proceedings interrupted, but she wasn't able to help her friend because the owner of Whitefish at once gave a pleased little nod, and launched into the remainder of his oration, which lasted a further ten minutes and caused Brenda to turn from alcoholic pink to an unattractive shade of pasty gray.

Beside her, Jessica sensed Jon's shoulders shaking, and she looked up anxiously, afraid he would give himself away. But his face was pulled into strictly sober lines, and only she guessed that the reason he was inspecting the pattern of the chair in front of him with such keen absorption was because if he once dared to meet her eyes he would burst out laughing.

When Mr. Sanegra finally brought his speech to a close with a few verbal flourishes about the joy of motherhood and the patter of little feet in the garden—both of which made Ben turn quite green—he immediately bustled over to interrogate the two newest arrivals.

"Well, well, well. So this is your young man," he declared, stating the obvious.

"Yes," agreed Jessica, who knew it wasn't obvious at all. "This is Jon Stuart."

"Delighted to make your acquaintance." Mr. Sanegra held out a pudgy hand which was immediately engulfed in Jon's large one.

"It's a pleasure to meet you too, sir," he replied, his voice a study in just the right mixture of confidence tempered with respect.

Then Jessica coughed, and when he glanced down at her she caught his eye, and it was impossible to miss the gleam of faintly malicious amusement he was concealing so well behind the reserved, respectful manner. To her horror *she* was now the one who found herself trying desperately not to laugh. Damn Jon Stuart! She might have known he wouldn't let her down—but she might also have known that he would manage to hold his end up in a way calculated to make *her* give away the game. And she was the one who prided herself on her acting!

She saw Brenda beckoning to her from across the room, and hurried over, abandoning Jon to the inquisition of her new boss.

"Who's *that*?" asked Brenda, without giving Jessica a chance to speak. "I thought you told me this morning that you haven't had a boyfriend since Richard."

"I haven't." She sighed. "I'm afraid Richard's put me off men for some time."

Ben, downing the remains of his glass, jerked his head in Jon's direction, and raised his eyebrows.

"Oh," explained Jessica airily, "that's just Jon."

Brenda's husband shook his head, shot her a look of mock alarm, and wandered back to the punch bowl. She noticed that all the female employees were contriving to gravitate toward the corner where Mr. Sanegra had buttonholed her bogus fiancé. They were followed, a little reluctantly, by their escorts, and soon Jessica and Brenda were alone on their side of the room. Even beady-eyed Mrs. Sanegra seemed more interested in her new employee's fiancé than she was in the employee herself.

Brenda pushed her short dark hair behind her ears, gaped at her old friend, and said in a tone of utter disbelief, ''Did you say 'just Jon'? Jess, there's no way that man could be 'just' anything. He's gorgeous! If I weren't married already I'd take him handed to me on a platter. Or even a paper plate,'' she added enthusiastically, glancing at Mrs. Sanegra's flimsy but time-saving hors d'oeuvres dishes. ''Aren't you really going to marry him next month?''

''No, of course not. He's a friend of Roger's, and I've known him most of my life. Don't you remember him?''

''Oh, *that* Jon. The one without an 'H.' I think he was away at university when you and I first became friends, and then later you had your own flat, and—oh, I don't know. Anyway, I never met him. *But*,'' she continued firmly, getting back to the subject at hand, ''the fact that you've known him all your life is no reason at all not to marry him. You'll have to do better than that, Jess. Does he run an international drug ring, rob little old ladies, beat his women...?''

''No,'' admitted Jessica ruefully. ''Mostly he makes me laugh.''

Brenda shook her head slowly from side to side. ''Jess,'' she said disgustedly, ''you're out of your mind.'' When Jessica didn't answer she asked curiously, ''What does he do, anyway? He looks like a pilot or a football player, or maybe a racing driver——''

''Try an accountant,'' Jessica suggested drily.

''Oh.'' Brenda paused, but only for an instant. ''But that's even better. He won't be off getting his neck broken.''

"I wouldn't count on it. He got that scar on his forehead when he overturned his canoe going down rapids that no one in their right mind would attempt. *He* says that was only in his reckless youth, but I'm not so sure. *And* he skydives. But that's beside the point, isn't it?"

"I don't see why."

"Because I don't want to marry him, for one thing. I've known him too long. Besides," she finished triumphantly, "he hasn't asked me."

"Hmm." Brenda shook her head again, and ran a hand absently over her swelling stomach. "You're slipping, Jess. At school you had every boy in the class panting over you."

"I did not. What about your Ben?"

"All right, not *quite* every boy, just most of them. What happened to Richard, by the way? I thought you two were almost engaged."

"We were." She turned her head away so that Brenda couldn't see her eyes. "But after the . . . the third time I found out he was seeing another woman I—well, I decided I'd been a fool long enough. I told you I'm a bit off men at the moment."

Jessica shrugged dismissively, but Brenda noted the hesitation, sensed the pain that her friend was trying so desperately to hide behind the offhand words and air of nonchalant indifference. She nodded sympathetically.

"I don't blame you, Jess. But don't let the right one get away."

Jessica was not given a chance to answer, because just then Jon broke away from the admiring throng which surrounded him, and came to ask her if he could get her a glass of punch.

She acquiesced at once, because she suspected he felt the need of something sustaining—and probably of something much stronger than the punch which nobody had bothered to offer them.

"Thank you," she said, keeping her face very straight as he presented her with a dubious glass of pale pink liquid. "Jon, I'd like you to meet Brenda Bonano."

"Of course. The friend I've heard so much about." Jon gave Brenda the sort of smile Jessica had always thought he reserved for elderly ladies and children. Apparently it worked on pregnant ladies as well, because by the time her friend slipped away a few minutes later Jessica could tell that Jon had made another conquest. She wondered why she felt vaguely resentful. Of course, she had always found him good company herself, but until tonight she hadn't really been conscious of the effect he had on others.

She gave a superior little smirk as he took a sip of punch, made a discreet face, and muttered something uncomplimentary about soda pop in disguise.

"Much better for you than strong drink, anyway," she stated sanctimoniously, sipping hers with a virtuous pretence of enjoyment.

"Hmm. And when did you join the local nunnery?" scoffed Jon. "You owe me one for this, Delaney."

"I always pay my debts," replied Jessica, looking so virtuous that Jon was tempted to shake her.

"And I always collect mine." His grey eyes traveled over her contemplatively, in a way that made her skin tingle unexpectedly. It was an odd sensation. She wasn't used to feeling uncomfortable around Jon—not that the tingling was unpleasant exactly, but...

She thought about asking in what form he usually collected his debts, but just then his lip curled in a curiously sensual way that did surprising things to her stomach— and she thought better of it.

"Jon, you mustn't let your fiancée monopolize you." A tall young woman with a lot of black hair came up beside them and grabbed Jon familiarly by the arm.

"I don't see why not," said Jon equably, disengaging it. "I do intend to marry her, you know."

Jessica choked into her drink, and had to be revived with a good deal of patting on the back. By the time she had recovered, the black-haired woman had disappeared, and Mrs. Sanegra was beside her looking concerned.

"You're not asthmatic, are you?" she asked, and Jessica had the impression that asthma was only slightly more acceptable than homicide in Mrs. Sanegra's opinion.

"No," she gasped, shaking her head vigorously. "I just swallowed my drink the wrong way."

Mrs. Sanegra continued to look disapproving.

"Entirely my fault, I'm afraid," Jon intervened smoothly. "I made a remark which upset Del—Jessica— and she happened to be drinking at the time. I'm sure it won't happen again." He flashed a rueful, apologetic and very white-toothed grin at the owner's wife, who was immediately won over.

"I'm sure it won't." She nodded, completely mollified. "Jessica, you're a very lucky young woman."

Jessica, who had been about to take another gulp at her drink, put it down hastily and mumbled that yes, she supposed she was.

This time it was Jon's turn to choke. "Can we get out of here soon?" he murmured, as Mrs. Sanegra reluctantly moved away, and the black-haired woman, with a blonde one in tow, began to edge back toward him. "My reservoir of charm and sociability is beginning to run exceedingly dry."

"But not your animal magnetism," muttered Jessica, as the blonde and the brunette swayed up beside him.

Jon's eyes sparked wickedly. "How kind of you to say so, Delaney. I didn't know you'd noticed."

"I haven't," she snapped, flinging her hand up in a gesture of frustration, and catching it in her amethyst necklace. Immediately the clasp loosened, and she watched in horror as the purple beads slid down the cleavage of her dress and disappeared between her small, neat breasts.

"Can I help?" asked Jon blandly, as she groveled helplessly with one hand, and tried frantically to prevent the necklace's further descent. "Privilege of the betrothed and all that."

"No!" yelped Jessica, back away from him with her arms wrapped around her chest, as her eyes searched anxiously for the exit. "No, you certainly can *not*."

She found the door into the hallway, and disappeared, unhappily aware that he was enjoying her discomfiture. If she hadn't known him better she would have sworn that as she left she heard him whisper softly "What a pity."

Once in the blue and gold bathroom with pink geese all over the wall, she rescued the necklace, shoved it into her bag, and took a long and very deep breath.

This brainwave of hers about enlisting Jon's help had *not* been one of her brighter ones. His behavior had been impeccable, he had done exactly what she asked him to do, and yet—and yet his presence was proving quite devastatingly distracting.

She returned to the party, found Jon holding court again, and as soon as it was decently possible suggested that they ought to leave. Pleading exhaustion, which occasioned knowing smiles all around, they thanked their host and hostess for a delightful evening, and beat a relieved retreat to Jon's car.

"Satisfied?" he asked as they sped down the darkened highway.

"What do you mean?"

"Was my performance up to standard? And, by the way, just in case you have any illusions, I have no intention of playing this role again. Under no circumstances will there be an encore."

"No, of course not. I wouldn't think of asking you to do it again."

When she saw that he had turned his head toward her, and was regarding her with a look of blatant skcepticism—which made her want to kick him instead of thanking him—she repeated sharply, "I really *wouldn't*. And yes. Thank you. Your performance was masterly. Much better than mine was." She had to admit it. "You carried it off beautifully."

Jon, as if he recognized how reluctantly the admission was made, bowed his head in mocking acceptance of her praise, and Jessica said with a mixture of irritation and contrition, "It wasn't really so very awful, was it?"

"I suppose not, if you consider being propositioned by two cocktail hostesses and a waitress with a dirty neck amusing."

"Were you really?" Jessica giggled. "Funny, I've never thought of you as the Casanova type before."

"So I've observed," he replied enigmatically.

A few minutes later they had pulled up outside the house near Centennial Park, and Jon was helping her out of his car.

They had just stepped into the front hall, shutting the door behind them, when the phone rang, and Nick ambled past saying he'd get it.

"Did you go to that party after all?" he asked over his shoulder as he groped for the receiver.

"We did," said Jon heavily, "and I'm beginning to think that getting engaged to your sister was *not* the most intelligent move I ever made."

Nick's eyes widened. "Getting engaged to—— Oh, hello, Mom. Where are you calling from?"

"It's Mother," said Jessica unnecessarily. "I think they're in Salzburg today."

Her voice trailed off as she heard Nick continue, "Did you say whose engagement? Oh, Jessica's, I guess. She just came home with Jon Stuart..."

A sound that was a cross between a whoop and a sob squealed over the wires so that, as Nick held the phone away from his ear, Mrs. Delaney's gurgling voice was audible across the hall.

"Hey!" cried Jessica, rushing toward her brother, and trying to grab the receiver. "Let me have that."

But, the moment he obligingly released it, the line went dead.

CHAPTER THREE

"NICK!" wailed Jessica. "What did you tell Mom *that* for? And why has she hung up?"

"She was in a phone booth," he replied casually. "Said someone was waiting to use it, and she'll be calling back tomorrow after she's told Dad the news." When he saw Jessica's stricken face, and her indigo eyes dark with horror, he added doubtfully, "Why? Is something wrong? *Aren't* you engaged to Jon, then?"

"Of course I'm not. I told you..." She hesitated.

"She told you she couldn't think of anyone she would less like to marry than me," said Jon impassively. "I believe there was also some mention of smug, patronizing old bores."

"Oh, Jon, you know I didn't mean..." Then, as the full enormity of what had happened overwhelmed her, she stopped worrying about Jon's sensibilities. She didn't think he had many, anyway. The real problem was that by some ghastly misunderstanding her mother was now firmly convinced that Jessica was engaged to Jon—and, judging from the noises she had heard trilling over the wires, Mrs. Delaney was more than pleased—she was ecstatic. Which would make the disappointment all the more shattering when Jessica explained the mistake. She had always been vaguely aware that her mother harbored fond notions of a union between the Stuart family and the Delaneys...

Oh hell, what a horrible muddle.

"Nick, how *could* you?" she groaned.

"It's not my fault," he protested, aggrieved. "*He* said getting engaged to you wasn't one of the more intelligent things he'd done."

"But you *knew* it was only for this evening," she accused him.

"I forgot," said Nick, giving the age-old teenage excuse. And in a sense Jessica knew it was true. Nick hadn't actually forgotten, but his mind was so absorbed by the Orange Peril parked in the driveway that nothing else held much meaning for him.

She groaned again.

"I'm sorry," said Jon stiffly. "My rather poor joke seems to have backfired. But you did bring it on yourself, Delaney. You always do."

Jessica's emotions, never far from the surface, erupted in a way that took both of them by surprise.

"You are a superior devil, aren't you?" she gibed, as the strain of her job interview, the party and now this latest calamity with her mother overcame her and exploded in a rush of indignant resentment at the only target she could find for her distress. "I was right the first time. You're a smug, self-satisfied jerk. If you hadn't told Nick we were engaged, Mother wouldn't be over there in Europe celebrating the news. And now you're trying to tell me it's all my fault!"

Something white and hot seemed to flicker in front of Jessica's eyes then, and she raised both fists to thump them down, hard, on his chest.

For a moment he just stood there, solid as a rock and unflinching, staring down at her hands which now lay still against the soft white cotton of his sweatshirt. Then his jaw tightened, and he caught her wrists swiftly in a firm grip.

Jessica stared up at him, suddenly unable to move. His eyes were stony, the line of his mouth forbidding. And he was very definitely not amused.

"Delaney!" His voice clipped her like a blow in the face. "That's enough. Now simmer down and start to behave like an adult instead of like a spoilt little girl. Because I've had about all I'm going to take from you for one evening."

Behind her, Jessica heard Nick mutter approval under his breath, and a moment later the door slammed and she and Jon were alone in the dimly lit hallway.

Jessica's body sagged a little as she looked into Jon's set face, but when she studied it more closely she saw that behind the authoritarian words there was still a stern but unmistakable affection. She also saw that the scarring across his forehead had gone quite white, and when his hands moved from her wrists to her upper arms she shivered. Suddenly all the unreasoning indignation drained out of her.

"Cold?" asked Jon softly, his voice no longer harsh and domineering, but filled with the quiet solicitude she had come to expect.

She shook her head. "No. No, I'm not cold. You— believe it or not—you scared me for a minute, that's all."

"Good," he replied unrepentantly. "A good scare won't do you any harm. How do you think I felt when you started to attack me like an ungrateful little wildcat?"

"Not scared," said Jessica with conviction.

"No. You're right. I felt bloody angry."

"I know. You wanted to hit me back."

"Damn right I did! So don't try it again, Delaney."

"I wasn't planning on it," Jessica assured him. "I'm sorry, Jon. That *was* a childish exhibition, and I honestly don't know what came over me. Especially when you've just done me such a good turn—with Mr. and Mrs. Sanegra, I mean.''

"Don't worry about it. You overreacted at the end of a bad day, nothing more.'' He smiled. "Like I said, just don't do it again.'' Softly his big hands moved and began to knead her shoulders. "Relax, Delaney. I'm sorry too— that my thoughtless joke has given your mother the wrong impression.''

Jessica sighed as she let the warmth of his caressing hands seep into her nerve ends, and she found herself drifting closer to the greater heat emanating from his body. There was something almost magnetic about his eyes now. They had her locked in an impossibly powerful grip.

"It's not your fault,'' she whispered unsteadily.

"No.''

Was he drawing her purposely toward him? She wasn't sure.

Slowly one big hand slipped beneath her long curls, cradling the back of her neck, and a remembered excitement snaked at the pit of her stomach. Remembered, and yet—different. This man wasn't Richard, this was Jon, who had never in his life looked at her the way he was looking at her now...except, perhaps, that once...

When her breasts touched the soft whiteness of his sweatshirt he drew in his breath, stared at her for a long, timeless moment, then muttered something which sounded like a curse—and let her go.

Startled and, in an obscure way, disappointed, Jessica staggered back. Automatically he reached out a hand to steady her, and then withdrew it abruptly.

"Party's over, isn't it, Delaney?'' he said cryptically. "Good luck with your mother tomorrow. And with your new job. Be good.''

He touched a finger briefly to her cheek, and before she could collect her wits to ask him if he wanted coffee he had closed the door none too quietly behind him.

Then she heard his car start up, and he was gone.

Unwillingly Jessica opened her eyes. The sun was flickering through a chink in the pink curtains, and it was Saturday morning. She blinked. Strange, she had been sure it would take her hours to fall asleep, but she must have been out like a light the moment her head hit the pillow.

She stared across the room at the curtains fluttering in the hot air from the furnace which they had been forced to turn on again last week. In spite of it there was an autumnal chill in the airy bedroom, and she pulled the blankets up around her chin.

What on earth had happened to her last night?—apart from the fiasco with her mother. Jon *had* been kind in his own way, and she had repaid him by attacking him like a—a wildcat, he had called her.

She smiled guiltily, remembering the feel of his chest beneath her fists and the quick sizzle of excitement she had felt when he touched her. An excitement she had never known with Richard. Or had she just forgotten? Perhaps she was only starved for male company.

Richard had always maintained she was starved for more than that, she recollected sadly, but then he had had his own hungers in mind. Hungers which, in the end, he had appeased with other women. Remembering, even after all this time, Jessica was surprised to feel tears stinging her eyes.

She dashed them away irritably. She *must* be feeling sentimental this morning. After all, she had always evaded Richard's attempts to maneuver her into his bed because, although she loved him, she had not, when it came right down to it, particularly wanted to sleep with him before marriage. Or with anyone else. It hadn't seemed right. But he hadn't understood that. Or perhaps, she reflected with a startling flash of perception, he had understood more than she knew, and hadn't cared. Looking back on it, she didn't think he had loved her at all.

Jessica tossed her head restlessly against the pillow, reminded of all those nights she had lain in the same bed crying herself to sleep, agonizing because Richard had betrayed her yet again. She would never forget those nights, that terrible hurt—and yet she knew that in a way the tears she was brushing away now had more to do with memory than actuality. Had Richard, after all, been right when he'd accused her of not loving him enough? It couldn't be...

She pushed the covers down, shivered, and pulled them up again. Richard was over. Jon was another matter entirely. She sighed. On top of everything else that had happened yesterday, an urgent case of unaccustomed—and misplaced—lust, for a man she considered a bit stuffy and far too familiar, had been altogether too much to take.

So she had hit him.

Gradually Jessica's tears evaporated, and her lips began to curve in a long, slightly sheepish smile. Jon had looked so—so *immovable*, standing there with a face like an angry rock, and then he *had* moved, with such lightning swiftness that he had actually frightened her for a moment. Imagine being frightened of Jon! She *must* have had an exceptionally bad day.

"And that's quite enough nonsense for one morning," she told herself decidedly, as she swung her legs out of the bed and sat up.

Her eyes fell on the mauve dress slung carelessly over a chair, reminding her of Jon's hands caressing the flimsy material and, to her surprise, because it was morning and she should have been over that midnight madness by now, once again she felt that shiver of excitement in her stomach. Had Jon felt a similar excitement? No, surely not. Frowning, she picked up the dress and hung it back in the wardrobe.

Happily her feeling of general discontent didn't last long. As she pulled on jeans and a sweater a few minutes later, once again she found herself smiling. In its own crazy way last night had been fun. Especially watching the smooth self-confidence with which Jon had carried off the deception. His Carol didn't know what she'd given up. Carol... For the first time Jessica felt a pang of curiosity about Jon's sloe-eyed singer. Curiosity, and something else. Something which she was damned if she was going to admit might be jealousy.

It certainly wasn't jealousy which moved her several hours later as she beetled around the supermarket loading up her shopping cart with hamburgers, eggs and ice cream, and almost ran over Jon's mother.

It was blind panic.

"Jessica!" Morag Stuart's fine-boned, still lovely face lit up as they narrowly avoided a collision. "Wonderful news. I'm so *very* pleased . . ."

"Er—news?" Jessica echoed doubtfully.

"Yes, dear. Your mother phoned me just over an hour ago."

Jessica felt her heart drop into her shoes. "Oh. I see. Wh-what did she say, Mrs. Stuart?"

"She told us your news, of course. My dear, Jon's father and I had no *idea*. We were *almost* resigned to his settling down with that Carol girl. *So* unsatisfactory, though. I mean, a *singer*!" Morag's rolling Scottish "R's" were more pronounced than ever this afternoon.

"Mrs. Stuart." Jessica's words came out as though a frog had lodged in her throat. "Mrs. Stuart, did Mother tell you that Jon and I—that we're...?"

"Of course she did, dear. She told us you're getting married. Soon, she said, and that you're having a nice big wedding at St. Mark's with at least four bridesmaids..."

"Oh," said Jessica faintly. "Four bridesmaids?" She gulped. "Um—what did Jon say, Mrs. Stuart?"

"Well, I haven't seen him yet, dear. You know he hasn't lived at home for years—yes, of course you do— but he's coming to pick me up in a few minutes when I've finished my shopping. His father's out of town on a sales trip, you know. Isn't that lucky? Not that Bruce is away, of course, but that Jon is picking me up. I shall give him a piece of my mind for keeping it all to himself. Wretched boy!"

Wretched boy? Jon? Jessica closed her eyes. Yes, Jon, who was *not* going to be amused when he discovered that he was supposed to be getting married to Jessica Delaney—at St. Mark's. With four bridesmaids. Much as Jessica loved her mother, who was apparently planning a mega-wedding from long distance, if she could have got her hands on her at this moment...

She fought down a craven inclination to bolt. Perhaps if she spoke quickly enough she could disabuse Mrs. Stuart of her fond but misguided notions before her son arrived on the scene.

"Er—Mrs. Stuart, I have to be going in a moment," she began. "I have an appointment. But I'm afraid I have to tell you..."

Morag wasn't listening. Jessica saw her face break into a beaming smile, and when she turned to look over her shoulder she knew she had left her explanations too late.

Bearing down on them, holding a large box of chocolates in his arms, was Jon. When he came to a halt beside them his eyebrows lifted inquiringly, and Jessica knew that any hope she had entertained of beating a discreet retreat to her car was already out of the question. Escape was effectively blocked off by a freezer full of strawberry ripple.

She sighed, and took a firm grip on her cart.

"Hello, Mother. Good afternoon, Delaney. We meet again." Jon's smile was easy and relaxed, but Jessica wasn't sure she trusted the gleam in his eye.

"Good afternoon." Jessica kept her gaze firmly on his chest, which today was covered by an open-necked white shirt which revealed the tough sinews of his throat. He never had felt the cold as much as she did.

"Jon! Why didn't you tell us?" Morag Stuart's voice was filled with accusation, but she couldn't keep the pleasure out of her eyes.

"Tell you what, Mother?" Jon stared at his parent, faintly puzzled.

"About your engagement, of course."

"Engagement?" His deep voice reverberated down the aisle, causing two large ladies in tracksuits to break off their conversation in order to listen.

"Engagement," repeated Morag severely.

Jon threw a disgusted glance at Jessica, and then asked softly, "What has Delaney been telling you this time, Mother?"

"Neither of *you* told us anything," replied Morag, aggrieved. "I had to hear the news from Meg, instead of from my own son."

"Meg?" Jon turned to Jessica. "Your mother?"

"She phoned an hour ago," said Jessica, staring fixedly at a speck of green fluff on his shirt.

"I see." Something in his voice made her look up quickly. He *sounded* disapproving and censorious—but his eyes met hers with a glimmer of provocation as he asked noncommittally, "What did Mrs. Delaney tell you, Mother?"

"That you're engaged, of course."

"To Carol?"

The provocation was now so blatant that Jessica had to clench her hands on the cart to stop herself from hitting him—again.

"No, of course not to Carol. Really, Jon, what *is* the matter with you?"

"Nothing, Mother. I guess I'm just not used to being engaged." His eyes were still on Jessica, and his face was as straight as a poker.

"Well, you'd better *get* used to it, hadn't you?" said Mrs. Stuart positively. "Of course, I'm delighted. But you ought to have told us, Jon."

"I didn't know myself," he replied, switching his bland gaze to the largest of the tracksuited ladies who, mouth agape, was moving closer.

"Oh, I see, and of course I was out last night, wasn't I?" said Morag, easily placated. "I suppose you weren't sure that Jessica would accept you."

Jessica glared at his carefully averted profile. "Jon..." she began threateningly.

"Yes, my dear?" His big body turned toward her abruptly, and she was struck anew by the catlike assurance with which he moved. Almost like the lion he resembled. The eyes that challenged her now had something almost feral about them, too.

"Jon, tell your mother——"

"She already knows," he said, resting his hip against the freezer.

"Knows...Jon, why are you doing this?"

He bent his head down then, and whispered into her ear, "I thought you *liked* playacting, my dear." She could feel his warm male breath against her neck, and for a fleeting moment she wondered what it would be like to feel his lips there. Then she started away as she saw Mrs. Stuart smiling at them indulgently, apparently convinced that Jon was murmuring sweet nothings to his love.

All right, she thought. All right, Jon Stuart, you got us into this mess, and now you can damn well get us out!

"I'm sorry, Mrs. Stuart," she said hastily, "but I've finished my shopping, and I do have that appointment. I'll—I'll see you soon."

"Yes, of course, dear. We'll get together to talk about the wedding. I am *so* pleased."

Jessica nodded, speechless, and hurried away down the aisle, almost knocking over a well-padded, still gaping tracksuit on her way, and although she couldn't see him she knew, without a shadow of doubt, that behind her Jon's full lips were parted in a mocking smile.

She hurried through the quick-service checkout, although she had by no means completed her shopping, and, still feeling flustered and angry, threw her one bag of groceries into the back of her car. Then she switched on the ignition, pressed down on the accelerator, and prepared to hurtle out of the parking lot before Jon and his mother reappeared.

The engine stirred, choked, muttered, and hiccuped into silence. She grumbled under her breath, and tried again. Nothing happened. Jessica groaned. Here she was, marooned in the supermarket parking lot, and in the next space over but one she could see Jon's New Yorker. A few moments later she could also see Jon pushing his mother's shopping cart, and moving unhurriedly toward her. Mrs. Stuart, still talking, was trotting beside him.

Jessica shut her eyes. When she opened them again Jon was on the other side of the door looking down at her.

"Trouble?" he asked lightly.

"My car won't start," replied Jessica, stating the obvious.

"Have you got gas in it?"

She glanced at the gas gauge, switched on the engine, and ground out through clenched teeth, "No."

"That might account for it, then, mightn't it?" he observed laconically. When she didn't answer he added, "Don't look at me in that tone of voice, Delaney. *I* didn't empty your tank."

Jessica's body drooped against the steering wheel. "I know you didn't. I meant to fill up on the way in, but I forgot."

"Apparently. You do cause yourself a lot of unnecessary trouble, don't you?"

"I've never done it before," she said indignantly. Then she glared at him because she was sure she wouldn't have done it this time either if he hadn't made such a goulash of her feelings last night. As a result of the disconcerting effect he had had on her, when she'd woken up this morning the practical matter of gas had been about the last thing on her mind.

"Mm." He stared at her thoughtfully. "I said don't look at me like that, Delaney. I thought we'd established that I'm not responsible for the fact that your car won't start." When she continued to glare up at him, he said resignedly, "Oh, come on, then. I'll drive you to the gas station after I've dropped off Mother."

Jessica contemplated telling him she could do without his help, thank you, but common sense came to the rescue, and reluctantly she opened the door.

"Thank you," she said haughtily, picking up her groceries and stalking past him toward his car.

Mrs. Stuart was beaming at them through the window, and Jon came up beside Jessica, and curled his arm lightly around her waist. "Mustn't shatter Mother's illusions, must we?" he murmured, dropping a feather-light kiss on her forehead.

Jessica tightened her lips and said nothing, mainly because she was incapable of speech. The touch of his fingers on her waist and that oh, so soft suggestion of what it might be like to kiss this man was acting like an aphrodisiac to her senses. She stumbled into the back seat like a sleepwalker who had no idea where she was going. So last night *hadn't* been just some temporary aberration. Her body, which seemed to have a mind of its own, was reacting to his virility—a virility which she had never consciously recognized—exactly as it had done the day before.

"Dear, oh, dear, I hope you won't miss your appointment," said Morag Stuart solicitously.

"No, no. It's all right. I'll still have time," muttered Jessica, making no attempt to satisfy her prospective "mother-in-law's" ill-concealed curiosity about her non-existent arrangements.

She sank back against the seat as Jon drove smoothly out of the parking lot and down the road. In the front, Morag was happily prattling on about how fortunate it was that they had been there at the right moment to help out her future daughter-in-law. Then she added guile-lessly that Jon seemed to have forgotten to give her the present he had bought her.

"Present?" stuttered Jessica.

"Yes, dear. That big box of chocolates my son has on the seat beside him. They must be for you."

"Oh, no..." began Jessica.

Without a word Jon extended an arm over the back of the seat and handed her the enormous, beribboned box.

"Oh, no, Jon," she said again. "You——"

"I know," he interrupted dryly, spinning to a stop in front of his mother's house. "I *shouldn't* have."

A few minutes later, as he pulled away again, now with Jessica sitting tensely beside him, he added, "I shouldn't have, but I didn't have much choice."

"Yes, you had. They're for Carol, aren't they? Why didn't you just tell your mother we're not engaged, and put a stop to this idiotic misunderstanding?"

"Because it's much more fun being engaged."

"But we're not... Oh, I see. You're trying to punish me, aren't you? For last night. This is your idea of a clever way to get your own back."

"And isn't it?"

She glanced sideways at him, and saw that his lips were curved in a smile of wicked satisfaction.

"No," she replied flatly, as she felt steam begin to hiss out of her ears. "It isn't. For one thing it's not fair to your mother, who thinks she's about to see Love's Young Dream consummated in white lace——"

"In public?" asked Jon interestedly, easing to a halt in front of a gas station.

"What do you mean, in pub—— Oh!" Jessica turned toward him, her unusual eyes flashing purple fire. "Jon Stuart, how dare you——?"

"How dare I what?" *His* eyes baited her, and the lips she was trying not to think about were lifted in a maddening little smile.

Jessica opened her mouth to deliver a sizzling put-down, then with an enormous effort of will she regained control. As she knew all too well, as long as his present mood persisted it would be impossible to get the better of Jon.

"I was referring to white lace and wedding veils," she replied with all the dignity she could muster. "Your mother is probably dreaming about them right now."

"Mm," agreed Jon. "I expect she is. Not to mention at least eight grandchildren."

"*Eight!* Jon, you can't do that to her. It's not fair."

Jon made a face and shuddered. "It wouldn't be fair to me either."

"Oh, stop it," she cried, exasperated. "I mean, it's not right to deceive her when you know she'll end up being disappointed."

"I don't know anything of the sort," said Jon shortly, the teasing light suddenly extinguished from his eyes. "Go on, out you get, Delaney. Fetch your gas."

"Aren't you going to be a gentleman and get it for me?"

"Who said I was a gentleman?"

Jessica stared at him, and after a minute decided he had a point. There was something decidedly primitive about the way he was returning her stare. His arm stretched along the seat with the fingers curled slightly, and he was leaning toward her in an attitude that was oddly disturbing. Suddenly he wasn't "good old Jon" any more, but some powerful creature poised to pounce at the first opportunity.

No, he certainly didn't look like a gentleman, and as she didn't want to be pounced on in full view of a mechanic and two pump assistants she jumped hastily out of the car.

Ten minutes later Jon delivered her back at the supermarket, and ten minutes after that she was pulling into the driveway of her house—right behind Nick's Orange Peril, which was surrounded by a throng of grease-stained teenage acolytes, all peering reverently down at the engine.

Still rigid with resentment at Jon's outrageous behavior—which, come to think of it, was most unlike him because he had always been the sensible one before—Jessica slammed her door shut behind her, waved quickly at the gang surrounding Nick's car, and didn't even realize that the cause of her indignation was standing right behind her until she had her key in the lock.

"You forgot your groceries," said Jon tersely. "Why in hell didn't you leave them in your car?" She could feel his breath again on her neck.

The surprise, coupled with a temper that was already near boiling point, caused Jessica to lose all sense of proportion. Jon had been baiting her all afternoon, and now he had found yet another excuse to disparage her. Clenching her teeth, and not even thinking about her audience, she lifted her foot and aimed a sharp kick at his shins.

But Jon had seen it coming and sidestepped quickly, so that Jessica overbalanced and fell against his chest. She clutched wildly at the bag of groceries he was holding in one arm and, as she did so, his other arm shot out and clamped her around the waist.

Behind them the greasy worshippers at Nick's mechanical shrine burst into raucous laughter.

"Match point to me, I think," murmured Jon, turning her firmly around to face the door. "Now for heaven's sake get inside and stop providing free entertainment for that gang of hooligans over there." He jerked his head at Nick's friends, who were waiting eagerly for Act Two of the drama.

"Oh, you—you..." Furious and almost speechless, Jessica turned the key in the lock, and stepped across the threshold.

At once she tried to shut the door on Jon and her groceries, but as usual he moved more quickly than she expected. One large foot was thrust into the opening, and his hand was touching her bottom as he pushed her ahead of him, kicked the door shut, and dumped the bag of groceries on a table.

Jessica glowered at him. "You keep your hands off me, Jon Stuart," she warned him.

"Certainly. If you'll promise to keep your hoofs off me."

"I'm not a horse," she grumbled, tossing her head and looking remarkably like a streamlined thoroughbred who was itching to begin the race.

"You could have fooled me," he muttered. He sounded angry, and the amused, patronizing air that had so inflamed her was no longer apparent.

She watched him, confused and much less anxious for revenge. Most of her annoyance had drained out of her with that unsuccessful attack on his shin. She glanced down and noticed that she was still holding his box of chocolates.

"Here," she said, handing it to him. "You can take this back now that your audience has gone."

His head was bent forward in a way that, oddly, she found endearing, and the gray eyes were hooded now as he replied curtly, "No. Keep them."

"But they're for Carol."

"They were. Now they're for you."

"But—why?"

"Because I want you to have them." His eyes weren't hooded any more, and he was leaning against the paneling with his arms crossed, looking surprisingly large and judgmental.

"I don't understand," she murmured. "Didn't you tell me last night that Carol was coming back today?"

"Yes, she is. Now stop looking a gift box in the mouth, and accept them graciously." He stopped looking judgmental and grinned suddenly. "You're not worried they'll turn you into a plump pudding, are you? There's no need."

"How do you know?" Jessica asked, suspicious of this unexpected change of mood.

"Because even if they did you'd be a thoroughly scrumptious pudding. Just the sort of pudding I'd want to taste—if you weren't you."

Jessica eyed him repressively. "You make me sound like one of those free samples of yogurt they hand out to shoppers in the supermarket."

Jon wrinkled his nose. "Yogurt? Revolting stuff."

Jessica laughed. "It is, isn't it? So, you see, I'd make a very unappetizing pudding."

"I'm not so sure about that." He eased himself away from the wall and took a step toward her and, awkwardly, Jessica reached behind her to put the box of chocolates on the table. Although he was still smiling there was something very purposeful in the way he moved.

She stood quite still, her hands clasped tightly behind her back, but, when he reached her, for a moment he just looked, his deep gray eyes moving slowly, languorously up over her hips and small breasts before coming to rest on her face. Then, without haste, he lifted his hands, placed them on her shoulders, and drew her against his chest.

Jessica's body tautened like a quivering violin string, and there was a hot, breathless tightness around her ribs. When his hand came to rest in her thick hair, pressing her cheek gently against the silkiness of his shirt, she made a soft, involuntary sound like a kitten purring.

"It's all right, Delaney," he murmured, his wonderful lips just touching the tip of her ear. "I won't beat you this time."

No, she knew he wouldn't. Jon had never hurt her. Teased her a little sometimes, threatened her when she pushed him too far, shouted at her—though rarely—but when she'd needed him he had always been there. He had been the rock to which she'd clung in every storm.

Now she stood reveling in an unaccustomed warmth, enjoying his closeness and the startling sensation that somehow she had come home. Then gradually, as he stroked his fingers through her hair, enfolding her with his quiet strength, she found herself wanting him to do more—more than... Oh, no. Surely—surely she didn't want Jon?

Hesitantly she lifted her head from his chest, saw the faint beginnings of dark gold stubble on his chin. Then she raised her eyes higher and found that his lips, those glorious, magic lips, were hovering just over hers.

Jon's skin seemed to darken as their eyes met, and he pulled in his breath sharply. When his arm began to move across her back she had a sense that it was almost with reluctance. Even so, although his grip on her was gentle, she knew that his mind was made up—that he wasn't about to let her go. Nor did she want him to.

Her hands, which all this time had been clasped behind her, opened virtually by themselves, and moved up to encircle his neck.

Jon drew another sharp breath, and then his free hand was tilting her chin up and, as Jessica closed her eyes, his firm mouth touched hers in a kiss of such startling sweetness that for a moment she thought she must be dreaming.

CHAPTER FOUR

JESSICA'S fingers tangled in the golden helmet of Jon's hair, liking the clean, springy feel of it, and as his kiss deepened, became more insistent, she felt his tongue begin to probe between her lips.

She let one hand drift down to caress the tight cords of his neck, relaxing them, and when his arms moved to draw her closer her body quivered with a growing need, and another soft little animal sound escaped her throat.

Then suddenly the dream was over.

Jon's body stiffened, and in the next instant his lips were withdrawn and he was holding her away from him, his eyes as hooded and remote as smooth gray stone.

"I'm sorry." His voice was remote too as he raised his arm to pass the back of a hand wearily over his dampened forehead.

Now he was almost a stranger she'd never met.

"Why?" said Jessica, whose head was still spinning in some rainbow cloud. "Why are you sorry, Jon?"

For a moment his hand covered his eyes, and when he let it fall again she saw that he looked more angry now than indifferent. Whether with her or with himself she wasn't sure.

"Because I've been a creep, I suppose," he said shortly. "I'd no right to take advantage of your..." He seemed to be searching for a word, and when it came it was both an accusation and a question. "Innocence."

Jessica smiled, a wry, inward sort of smile. So Jon was at least vaguely aware that the girl he had always regarded as a crazy kid might possibly turn out to be a woman.

"Yes," she replied dryly. "I suppose you could call it that."

A look that was almost embarrassment flared in his eyes, and disappeared. "I'm sorry," he said stiffly, "I didn't mean to imply——"

"Yes, you did," retorted Jessica with conviction. "You've just discovered I know how to kiss—a possibility which hadn't crossed your mind before—and you started to wonder if perhaps I had other, hitherto unacknowledged talents. Didn't you?"

"Don't be vulgar."

"And don't you be stuffy. There's nothing vulgar about honesty. Oh, and incidentally, my love life isn't any of your business, Jon, dear."

"I didn't say it was. Not that it matters, as you've just told me you don't have one. Oh, and *incidentally*," he added with exaggerated mimicry, "there is nothing stuffy about expecting a little decorum from a young lády I've gone to a lot of trouble for over the years."

"Good grief!" Jessica gaped at him, struggling to find words. "Did you really say 'decorum'?" she managed at last, in a thin, rather strangled voice.

Jon continued to stare down at her, arms folded on his chest, lips rigid with disapproval.

Jessica returned his stare, swallowed, made a frantic effort to control herself, and then gave up and burst out laughing.

For a moment he didn't react at all as his eyes fastened on her gleeful face. Then slowly his brow cleared, and after a moment the taut lips parted in a grin that was decidedly sheepish.

"I did sound like a pompous ass, didn't I?" he admitted, not sounding in the least penitent. The grin broadened and became teasing instead of sheepish. "Sometimes, Delaney, I have a great deal of trouble remembering that you've reached the age of consent."

Jessica heard the amusement in his voice, and knew he still didn't really believe she was a woman. Or if he did it was only as a child in a woman's body. And suddenly she didn't feel like laughing any more. Just the opposite. She felt confused, resentful, unhappy in an obscure sort of way—and very definitely fed up with Jon.

"Oh, never mind," she snapped, lifting her head and looking him straight in the eye. "I know you can't help being a pompous ass, Jon Stuart. I think you were born that way. And don't worry about that kiss. It wasn't bad for a puritanical accountant. But I've known better."

She caught just a glimpse of his face, white with surprise and accusation, and his eyes, dark gray and misted with smoke, before she turned her back on him, wishing she hadn't spoken.

"Thanks for driving me," she added tightly, feigning an unusual fascination with the floor.

"Jessica! Stop that."

His voice snapped at her, whiplike, but she only hesitated for a second before marching deliberately in the direction of the stairs.

Jon took two strides and caught her arm.

"Jessica! Where the hell do you think you're going?"

"To my room," she said curtly.

"Don't be ridiculous. Surely even *you* don't go to bed at this hour. Although it might be a damn good place for you!"

"You mean that in a 'purely paternal' sense, of course," she taunted him.

"Fraternal. If I were your father, right now you'd be getting a lot more than bed."

"How fortunate for me you're not, then," she replied with icy sweetness.

Jon swore. "Jessica, look at me."

"No. I'm going upstairs. And don't bother following me, I've got work to do."

"Don't flatter yourself," he growled. "The only reason I'd think of following you would be——"

"I know. To put me to bed. But *not* the way you bed your Carol," she jeered, beginning to make her way up the stairs.

"For pity's sake, you're asking for it, Delaney."

Jessica heard the barely controlled violence, the tone which he had never used with her before, and she recognized that she had almost gone too far. A tactical retreat at this point was the only intelligent option.

"Thanks again for the ride," she shouted over her shoulder, moving hastily out of his way.

Behind her she heard a number of explicit phrases which she didn't imagine were taught as part of the standard accountancy curriculum. And at this moment Jon did *not* sound chartered. In fact, when he crashed his fist against the banister, slammed the front door so hard that the whole house shook, and roared the engine of his car in exactly the same way Nick did, he sounded like a remarkably angry man.

From her window Jessica watched him go. It was raining now, a thin, dismal rain, and a leaf drifted off the maple at the bottom of the garden and flattened itself against the pane, a faded reminder of brighter, sunnier times.

She bent forward and rested her head against the glass, feeling as dreary and gray as the weather. What had happened today to spoil their easygoing friendship? What had made her say those awful things? Things she didn't mean, because she would never deliberately hurt

Jon. Not that she had, she supposed. He had seemed more livid than hurt. The trouble was, that kiss, chaste as it had been, had awakened something in her—if not in him—something she was almost afraid of. And it was an out and out lie she had told him about having experienced better. Because she hadn't.

"I'm sorry, Jon," she whispered to the empty room. "I can't blame you for being angry. I'd like to, but I can't."

She closed her eyes, long lashes accentuating the unusual paleness of her cheeks. Why, oh, why had this happened? Why had Jon kissed her? Not because he took her seriously as a woman. He'd made that clear. She sighed. Just circumstances, then. He'd been holding her, and at that moment she must have *felt* to him like a woman. Yes, that had to be it.

The question now, though, she acknowledged as she stared glumly at the rain, was why on earth did she care? Had cared to the point of doing everything in her power to hurt him for making what, after all, had only been a casual joke about what in his view was her immaturity.

Surely—oh, no, surely she hadn't—been on the brink of loving Jon? She didn't want to, she *mustn't*, love anybody yet. Not with the wound of Richard's betrayal still raw and chafing. Fidgeting with a corner of the curtain, she reflected that there had never been anyone serious before Richard. And he had turned out to be a first-class, award-winning mistake. A mistake whose memory made her burn with shame whenever she thought about how often he'd deceived her—and how she had foolishly believed his promises that it wouldn't happen again. And, because of that, she didn't want to love anyone else for a long time. Especially not Jon. She needed Jon as her dependable, imperturbable friend.

And now perhaps she had hurt him.

The rain beat on the window, dislodging the faded leaf, and jolting Jessica out of her fog of self-recrimination. Damn it, it *was* partly his own fault! He had been so maddeningly patronizing, and he *would* persist in treating her as a child, just because she sometimes behaved with less than schoolmarmly dignity. She made a face, saw it reflected in the glass, and grinned irrepressibly, feeling an instant lightening of her spirits. To hell with dignity! It was time to stop this useless musing and moping.

Jumping to her feet, she ran downstairs to start supper. Life and food and Nick's insatiable appetite would go on. And from now on she would concentrate on writing. At least the Reverend Michael McGillicuddy and Colonel McWhirter were unlikely to let her down, and if they tried to she would write them out of her story.

It was only as she finished setting the table and began to heat plates in the stove that she remembered that Jon had called her "Jessica." He only did that when he was *very* angry.

Unbidden, a picture came into her mind of dark blond hair above a scarred forehead, and long legs that seemed to stretch up out of sight...

"Damn you, Jon Stuart," she said out loud, wearily and without much conviction. "You sure know how to drive a woman crazy."

"Hey, you've sure got it in for old Jon, haven't you?" remarked Nick's cheerful voice as the door slammed loudly behind him.

"I have not 'got it in'..." began Jessica. Then she stopped. What was the use?

"That's good," he replied carelessly, "because Mom called again, and she'd been buying you all kinds of pewter."

"Pewter? What for?"

"For a wedding present." Nick pulled out a chair and straddled it, his arms hanging over the back.

"Nick!" wailed Jessica. "Didn't you tell her...?"

"I didn't have the heart, and, anyway, she didn't give me time."

Jessica groaned. "Where *is* Mother? Can I call her?" Her voice was exaggeratedly controlled.

"On the way to Munich, she said. She'll call in a couple of days. Oh, and she's buying you beer tankards."

Jessica groaned again.

"Don't you like tankards?" he asked innocently.

His sister cast him a look of acute disfavor which had no visible effect on him, and dumped a frying pan wearily down on the stove.

"Delaney?"

It was early Monday morning, and Jessica was back at the supermarket collecting all the things she'd neglected to buy on Saturday.

Sunday had been a day of rest, of regret for what might have been—and writing. As she had anticipated, the Colonel and the Reverend Michael had successfully banished Jon from her thoughts—for some of the day.

Now, just when she was sure she had put Saturday out of her mind, here he was, standing squarely in front of her with his hands on her cart so that she couldn't move it—but he wasn't looking as sure of himself as usual.

As she stared at him, to her utter confusion, she was suddenly and devastatingly aware that the question she had asked herself earlier had been answered. She might not be in love with Jon, but she most *certainly* was not in love with Richard any longer.

"What are you doing here?" she asked, knowing she was being rude, but too shattered by this revelation to care. "Why aren't you chartering your accounts?"

Jon's full lips, which had parted in the beginnings of a smile, clamped shut immediately. Then they opened again, barely, to reply without inflection, "My working hours are nobody's business but my own, Delaney. And possibly Brad's. If you must know, I'm escorting Mother again. Dad won't be back until tomorrow."

"Oh." Jessica's eyes darted uneasily sideways. She didn't think she could face Morag Stuart just at the moment, especially as she didn't know what Jon had told her.

"Don't worry," he assured her, correctly divining her thoughts. "She's totally absorbed with an improving display of yogurt."

Jessica glanced up at him suspiciously. Was there a glimmer of laughter in his eyes?

"Oh," she said again.

There was silence between them, and after it had gone on a fraction too long she mumbled awkwardly, "I have to get on with my shopping, Jon, if you don't mind."

"But I do mind."

"That's too bad, isn't it?" she said evenly.

"Is it?" He was looking at her with an odd, reflective and possibly retaliatory look in his eyes.

"Jon, really—let me pass. *Please*." She wasn't pleading. The "please" was unmistakably sarcastic.

Jon shook his head. "Only if you'll promise to have lunch with me. I want to talk to you."

"But I don't think *I* want to talk to *you*."

"I don't altogether blame you. But if you want to avoid my mother, which I know you do, you don't have much choice, do you?" He was definitely smiling now.

but it was an implacable sort of smile, and his tone left her in no doubt that he meant it.

She cast a harried glance behind her, and thought she saw Morag Stuart negotiating the end of the aisle.

"All right," she muttered resentfully. "What time?"

"I'll pick you up around one."

Jessica nodded. "Does any *work* ever get done around your office?" she inquired waspishly, seizing the last word the moment Jon released her cart.

"Not a hell of a lot since Friday," she heard him call after her as she hurried past a row of jams and jellies.

She hadn't got the last word, after all.

Now what did he mean by *that*? She closed her eyes for a moment, and cannoned straight into the large lady in the tracksuit whom she had nearly mown down two days before.

"Well done, you've finally got her," purred Jon's voice in her ear.

The large lady was too flabbergasted to say anything, but Jessica flushed to the roots of her hair, and mumbled an apology. Then she grabbed her cart again, and fled.

Finally got her, indeed! Jessica giggled. By the time she reached the car her shoulders were shaking, so she collapsed on to the front seat, buried her face in her arms, and gave way to unrestrained laughter.

In spite of everything she was *glad* he wanted to talk to her, because to her own consternation she was beginning to realize that life with no prospect of being around Jon Stuart might turn out to be remarkably dull.

The phone was ringing as she pushed open the door with her hip and swerved into the hallway with three precariously balanced bags of food.

"Rats!" she muttered, dumping the bags onto the living-room sofa and practically falling back on top of the phone. "Mother, you do pick the most wonderful times..."

But it wasn't her mother.

It was Richard. And the revelation that had come to her in the supermarket was confirmed.

The voice that had once caused her to go limp with delight and love now meant nothing to her at all.

"Oh, it's you," she said, recapturing her breath with an effort. "What do you want?"

"What have I always wanted?"

"Richard, don't start that again. It's over."

"Jessica, love——"

"I'm not your love. Not any more."

"Ah, but you could be. I miss you."

"No, you don't. I heard you broke up with Ilona, but that doesn't mean I'm available as a backup. Not this time."

"Jessica——"

"Look, I do wish you well, Richard, but I don't want to see you again. I meant that five months ago, and I still mean it. So right now I'm going to hang up."

"Jess——"

His words were cut off abruptly as Jessica placed the receiver quietly back on its stand.

She stood staring at it for a moment, then shook her head and passed a hand over her eyes. Richard, today of all days, was just about the last person she wanted to hear from. But at least she knew that now. The wound had healed. The shame and the memory of pain were still there, but she really did wish him well. And, she realized with relief, she didn't have to worry much about hurting his feelings, because now that her eyes were opened she understood that he was too self-absorbed to be hurt much, except in the very shallowest sense.

She glanced at her watch, and then hurried back into the living room to collect the groceries, most of which had tumbled onto the floor.

Jon showed up at one o'clock precisely, looking expensive and impressive in a severe dark gray three-piece that made every slight movement of his body appear as though he meant business.

Jessica, noting that the color of his suit matched his eyes, found that her mouth had suddenly gone quite dry.

"Oh," she murmured, "I thought you weren't working today. You look as though you've just come out of a meeting."

"I have. Contrary to your assumptions, my dear, I do occasionally find it necessary to earn a living."

Jessica smiled. "I know you do. But you make me feel very underdressed in this jumpsuit and jacket."

"Underdressed?" He raised an eyebrow. "Would I were so lucky. But I suspect it would take an assault team to get past that array of pink zippers and buttons. Nonetheless, you look very charming, Delaney." He offered his arm. "Shall we go?"

So now he was all smiles and banter again, after that display of patronizing bossiness the other day.

Jessica took his arm doubtfully, and as they walked toward his car she was frowning. She wasn't at all sure she appreciated his blatant innuendoes. Not after the way he had kissed her, turning her world upside down for a few intoxicating seconds, and then reverted without visible effort to the brotherly, slightly overbearing role he had played for most of her life. So had he changed his mind again, by any chance? Was he insisting on this lunchtime tryst now because of some lingering recollection of that very unfraternal kiss? In spite of Carol?

If he was, he had another think coming.

But as he guided her into the dining room of one of Thunder Bay's best hotels, and made sure that she had a good view of Mount McKay rising in stark, terraced emminence behind the level plains of the Kaministikwia Delta, Jessica saw that there was no suggestive speculation in the way he looked at her now, but only a kind of amused, appreciative contemplation—as though he wasn't quite sure whether she was his Delaney still, or some unfamiliar bird of bright plumage he had mistakenly caught in his net.

She wasn't sure why, but his look made her uncomfortable, and because of that she felt she had to keep up an inconsequential stream of chatter that would prevent him from becoming too personal.

"It's a beautiful legend, isn't it?" she said brightly, nodding her head at the flat-topped mountain across the plain.

"What? What legend?" Amusement changed rapidly to incomprehension.

"The one about the chapel on Mount McKay. Don't you remember? When a plague of black birds swooped down out of the sky and devoured all the Ojibway's crops?"

"Oh," said Jon. "That legend. Yes, I do remember. A bad winter followed the birds, and soon there was no food for the people..."

"That's right, and they couldn't fish through the ice because there was nothing left for bait. So just when it looked as though the whole tribe would starve the chief's daughter took her father's hunting knife and cut strips of her own flesh for the men to use as bait—and because of her they were all saved from starvation."

"Except the chief's daughter," he said dryly.

"No, she died," agreed Jessica. "But a visiting priest blessed her, and had the men build a chapel in her memory."

"That must have been a great consolation," murmured Jon.

"But don't you think it's a beautiful story?" she persisted.

"No, I don't. Delaney, were you a vampire in some previous incarnation, by any chance?"

Jessica shook her head disgustedly. "There's no romance in your soul," she complained. "I suppose *you* think beauty is a nice, neat column of figures."

"Not necessarily, although I'll concede that I do find the thought of a neat column of figures more appealing than a neat strip of bleeding flesh."

Jessica opened her mouth to tell him, priggishly, that he obviously had no conception of the beauty of heroic self-sacrifice. Then she saw that he was smiling at her again—a slanting, seductive smile that she knew had no connection whatever with the legend of the chief's brave daughter.

Her attempt to keep the conversation impersonal was about to fail—dismally, she suspected—because the speculative look was back in his eyes, along with that hypnotic smile.

"Delaney," he said softly.

"Mm?"

"Forgive me?" Suddenly he was reaching across the table to take her hand.

"Forgive you for what?" she asked warily, pulling it away again because his touch was making her head spin alarmingly.

"For not kissing you in the style to which you've become accustomed." The gray eyes regarded her with faint malice.

Jessica gasped and lowered her eyes quickly, even though she was sure that was precisely what he wanted her to do.

"I—that wasn't true," she muttered, taking a quick sip of her soup, and almost choking.

"What wasn't?" inquired Jon equably. "You mean you *haven't* become accustomed——?"

"No! I mean, yes. I meant I haven't had better kisses. I don't know how——"

"Don't you now? You could have fooled me." He leaned back in his chair and gave her a slow, contemplative and very irritating smile.

Jessica dropped her spoon with a clatter. "Jon, don't."

"Don't what?"

"Don't laugh about it. You *were* your usual overbearing self on Saturday. And you *will* keep treating me as a child. But I—I know I shouldn't have said that about Carol."

"No, you shouldn't," he agreed.

"And I shouldn't have called you a puritanical accountant, either——"

"You should if it's true."

"But it isn't. Jon, when you kissed me, it—it was quite different from . . ." She paused, not knowing how to put it.

"From Richard?" he suggested dryly.

"Well, yes, but I mean—it was more than that." She lifted her head suddenly, and looked at him. "It was nice."

"Nice?" The corner of his mouth twisted. "That's damning with faint praise, Delaney."

"Oh, stop it!" If she hadn't been sitting down Jessica might have stamped her feet. "You brought me here because you said you wanted to talk to me, and you've done nothing but try to aggravate me ever since."

"Am I doing a good job?" he asked, raising his eyebrows inquiringly.

She clenched her teeth. "You know you are. And if you don't cut it out I'll take back that apology I'm trying to make."

"Are you making an apology?"

"No," she said caustically. "I'm looking for something suitable to throw."

He grinned. "That sounds more like my Delaney."

The grin was so infectious and disarming that, despite herself, Jessica found she was succumbing to its charm. "Truce," she said, smiling resignedly. "And yes, I am apologizing. For making uncalled-for remarks about your—your relationship with Carol, and for deflating your male ego. It's a sincere apology, by the way, and if you'd only stop baiting me——"

"I'm sorry."

Jessica stopped in mid-sentence. "What did you say?"

"I said I'm sorry. You're right. I have no business at all to tease you about something as serious as kissing."

Jessica glanced at him suspiciously, but his face was dead sober, and he went on as if he meant every word. "I had no business to suggest that a spell in bed would be good for you, either."

"Jon, you're still doing it."

"Telling you that bed . . .? No. Sorry." He pulled his face into even more solemn lines. "Delaney, I *do* realize you're a grown woman—most of the time. And I agree that I have no right to tell you how to behave."

"You always have, though," Jessica replied with deep gloom.

"Mm." He smiled thoughtfully. "It's hard not to when you keep pulling stunts like that nonsense out at Whitefish."

"I suppose so," she admitted grudgingly. "But you're *not* my brother, you know, Jon."

"No. I've come to that conclusion myself."

"You have?"

"I'm afraid so. With no justification whatever I have found myself wanting to change the shape of Richard's elegant nose for him. I have also, several times, felt an inexcusable urge to wallop you soundly before sending you off to bed. Not necessarily alone. And not, I think, with a particularly fraternal attitude."

Jessica gaped at him, stunned, then stared down into her soup. What did he mean? Was he teasing her again? Knowing Jon, it was quite possible. And yet... Her mind skimmed briefly back to Richard. If *he* had made an admission like that she would have been hard put to it not to punch him on what Jon called his "elegant nose." But somehow, coming from Jon, the words had a different effect on her entirely, and the images they conjured up made her mildly indignant, yes, but at the same time...

"Not necessarily alone", he had said. No, he *couldn't* have meant what she was thinking...

She knew his eyes were riveted on the top of her head, and eventually she was forced to look up. He was smiling, a cool, subtle smile. "I wouldn't worry about it," she said, her cheeks glowing a soft shade of rose. "I'm sure all you were feeling was your usual urge to boss me around. After all, you've got Carol."

He shook his head. "As a matter of fact, I haven't."

The waiter brought their salads then, and it was several minutes before Jessica was able to ask the question that was burning the tip of her tongue.

"What did you mean about Carol? I thought you two were getting married."

"Heaven forbid." He raised his eyes to the high, painted ceiling. "No, Carol and I had certain...tastes in common..." He smiled cynically. "But marriage was never on the cards."

"I see. So now you're tired of her, I suppose?" Jessica was unable to keep her disapproval from showing. She remembered all too vividly the ease with which Richard had forgotten his promises.

Jon shrugged. "Maybe I am. But I believe she's equally tired of me. We've seen very little of each other lately."

"But those chocolates..."

"They were just a friendly parting gift. She phoned me to say she'd be in town overnight before leaving for Montreal in the morning. We arranged to meet for a farewell drink, as a matter of fact. Carol and I are still excellent friends, we enjoyed each other for a while, but she had a career..." He shrugged again. "Neither of us thought of it as permanent."

"Your mother did."

"Mother has a great imagination."

Jessica picked up her fork, and began to push lettuce around on the plate. "Jon," she said carefully, "haven't you ever thought *anyone* might be permanent? I mean, you had other...liaisons before Carol. Lots of them," she added, remembering an endless procession of glamorous, high-spirited and, on the whole, rather dizzy ladies—all very like Carol.

To her surprise, his body tensed suddenly. "You mean have I ever succumbed to the nesting instinct? Certainly not. I've always taken care not to." The words were glib, but his eyes were flat, revealing nothing.

Well, she thought, it made sense. Jon's life had always followed exactly the path he had mapped out for it. Unwanted emotional entanglements wouldn't fit into his scheme of things at all. Hence the glamorous ladies. But it might do him good to find out what it felt like to care about someone—not *always* to have things his own way...

"Are you sure you and Carol couldn't patch things up?" she asked, wondering why she hated the suggestion. "I mean, you've been together for quite a while..."

"Our decision to part company is mutual," he said flatly. "And final."

So was the tone of his voice.

"And now that we've got that straight," he continued amiably, "what about you and your Richard?"

"What about us?"

"Are *you* considering patching things up?"

"No." Her reply was equally flat and final.

"And there's no one else?"

She felt herself bridling. "If you mean do I make a habit of flitting——"

He shook his head. "No, no. That's not what I mean. I have no idea what you make a habit of, and you're quite justified in telling me your love life is none of my business."

"I don't *have* a love life—as you once pointed out."

"Good. In that case I'm unlikely to get my face smashed if I ask you to come out to Nipigon with me on Sunday. It's business, but it shouldn't take long." He smiled, the old engaging smile that she was used to. "Come with me. Afterward perhaps we can have dinner."

Jessica watched the broad shoulders shift under his jacket, noticed the muscles of his chest which no thin shirt could quite conceal. And she knew he wasn't remotely concerned about getting his face smashed. She also knew, without wanting to believe it, that she was feeling the first faint stirrings of desire—desire for this big man who, until last Friday, she had never even thought about except as a comfortable convenience.

A convenience, she recollected, who had just broken off with his girlfriend. At least he said they had broken off. And, if the break was final, did he intend to replace Carol with Jessica now that it had at last occurred to him that she might be a grown-up, willing woman? If so, the worm had turned, and this time *she* was the convenience.

"No, I can't..." she began.

Jon's hand snaked across the table and caught her wrist, and his gray eyes seemed to hold her, too, in a velvet-soft, inescapable grip. A grip from which she didn't *want* to escape, she realized. Just for a second she felt like an anesthetized butterfly on a board, and in that moment she heard herself saying, "All right, Jon. Yes. I'll come."

Afterward she wondered what she had done. She didn't want any complications in her life at this point. She had just recovered from Richard, and she wanted to get on with her book. But that hadn't been a casual invitation on Jon's part. At least, she didn't think so. He often had business in the small towns around Northern Ontario but, as far as she knew, he always made the journeys alone.

That meant there was a purpose behind his invitation, and she was very well aware that something in their relationship had changed since he had agreed to play the part of her fiancé. Good old Jon was no longer the surrogate brother. He had suddenly, and mysteriously, turned into a dangerously attractive man.

She wasn't sure what he felt about her.

What had happened to the two of them? They had known each other forever, she had always loved him in the way one loved someone who has been an integral part of one's childhood, but this thing that was between them now—it was different. And she wasn't sure she was ready for the change. Especially if he was just looking for a handy replacement for Carol. She didn't think she could handle that at the moment. Not from her reliable rock. Not from Jon.

On the other hand, perhaps, as usual, her imagination was running away with her. Maybe it *had* been just a friendly invitation.

Everything had happened so fast that she couldn't really take it all in...

As the week passed, and she began to adjust to her new job and to getting up at the uncivilized hour of five a.m., Jessica hadn't much time to brood about the unexpected problem of an old friend turned into a possible lover. But when her mother called again at the end of the week the problem returned with a vengeance. Because once again Nick fielded the call and, with casual disregard for his parents' bank balance—Meg Delaney was now buying linen in Ireland—neglected to break the news to her that his sister's engagement was a myth.

"And *what* a myth!" moaned Jessica, as she gazed gloomily into her wardrobe on Sunday morning. There wasn't really a chance of Jon's becoming a lover, let alone her betrothed. True, she had felt a fleeting attraction—apparently he had too—but that was just because they hadn't seen much of each other lately. She had had Richard, he had had Carol. When they were called on to pretend to an engagement it had been a novelty. But novelties inevitably wore off.

She sighed, wondering why this sensibly realistic appraisal left her with an empty feeling somewhere in the region of her stomach. Jon would probably tell her it was because she just wasn't used to being sensible. But that wasn't true. She had always been sensible when sense was really needed, and the regret she felt now had nothing to do with prudence and practicality. It had to do with her feelings about an old and valued friend. Feelings which she didn't even want to understand.

"And that's enough of that, Jessica," she told herself, as she grabbed decisively at a pair of purple pants and a matching purple print blouse. "Stop feeling sorry for yourself. There's no excuse for it. You'll go out with Jon today, have a pleasant afternoon being your old cheerful self, and then everything will go back to normal."

But when Jon arrived an hour or so later she almost groaned out loud. Normal? What could possibly be normal about the way her heart started executing high kicks the moment he walked into the room? Or about the way he crossed straight over to her, caught her around the hips, and planted a boisterous kiss just below her right earlobe?

"Jon!" she gasped. "What do you think you're doing?"

"Kissing a dingbat," he replied smugly.

"That's not good enough..."

"No? I'll try to do better." Wicked white lights sparkled in the cloudy gray of his eyes as, very purposefully, he moved an arm around her waist to pull her closer.

"Jon! Stop it. This isn't like you. Couldn't we *please* go back to being the way we were?"

"How do you know it isn't like me?" There was a constraint in his voice now, but he released her at once, making her feel oddly bereft.

"Because—because—— Oh, Jon, you were always the one I could count on. Please don't turn into someone I don't even know."

"All right, Delaney. If you say so. I wasn't going to rape you, you know." He turned away from her, and as she stared at his profile she saw lines at the corner of his mouth that she hadn't noticed before. And she wondered why he had suddenly withdrawn. He couldn't really have thought she was accusing him of attempted assault—could he?

She sighed. The old Jon had never been withdrawn or enigmatic. He had been comfortable. This Jon, in tight black jeans and a soft black sweater, who was talking to her about rape—he wasn't comfortable at all.

But he *was* magnificent.

Yes, but you don't need magnificence, she reminded herself. What you need, Jessica Delaney, is the nice, solid, reliable, ordinary, *safe* old friend you've always had.

She wasn't sure why that was so important, but it was.

True to his word, John kept his eyes on the road, didn't tease her, and behaved like the calm, unemotional pillar of sober accountancy she'd said she wanted. And Jessica wondered why she was disappointed.

"How's the job?" he asked conversationally, and not as if he particularly cared.

"It's fine. Mr. Sanegra's away most of the time. He has an office furniture business in Fort William as well as the hotel. And Mrs. Sanegra is quite happy to leave the front desk to me."

"No managerial interference, then?"

"No. But those two hostesses keep asking me about you. One of them wants to know where you live. Shall I tell her?"

"Not if you value your pretty skin."

"You terrify me. Didn't you make a pass at them, then?"

"In front of my fiancé? You have a flatteringly high opinion of my integrity, Delaney. And no, I did not make a pass at them. At the risk of being accused of bragging, I can assure you it was the other way around.''

He spoke lightly, but Jessica heard an edge of irritation. She didn't blame him. Although she had only recently come to see it, Jon Stuart was a very attractive man. He wouldn't need to make passes at eager hostesses.

"I believe you.'' she said quickly. "Jon...?''

"Mm?'' He cast a dubious eye at a drop of rain on the windshield.

"Jon, I'm sorry it's over between you and Carol.'' She wasn't sure what she'd meant to say, but it certainly hadn't been that.

"Don't be,'' he said shortly. "Carol and I suited each other for a while, but all unsatisfactory things come to an end, and now it's over.''

"You really don't mind, do you?'' She glanced at him almost shyly, and for the first time since he had started the car he smiled.

"No. It's a relief. And Mother's delighted. She regarded poor Carol as very dim marriage material.''

Jessica laughed. "I know. She told me.''

"And she thinks you're *much* more suitable. I can't imagine why.'' Jon's eyes stayed blandly fixed on the road.

"Oh, dear.'' She twisted toward him. "Jon, she phoned me *twice* at the beginning of the week. You *have* told her now, haven't you? That we're not——''

"What do *you* think?''

Jessica didn't know what to think, but she saw from the set of his jaw that she wouldn't get more of an answer out of him than that, so she gave him an indignant glare which he didn't see, and sank resignedly back against her seat.

Half an hour later they pulled into Nipigon and came to a stop in front of a big white house in the residential section just below the town's scenic lookout.

Jessica chose to wait outside, enjoying the clouds over Nipigon Bay and the changing hues of the trees. In a very short time Jon was back, and as he slid into the seat beside her it started to rain.

"That was quick," remarked Jessica. "Why did you have to come all the way out here on a Sunday?"

"Client's an old acquaintance, and I enjoy the drive. I usually contrive to come on a working day, but I couldn't arrange it this time."

She nodded. "Yes, I see."

What she really saw was that Jon Stuart, sober, successful businessman, felt the constraints of being office-bound on occasions—and had found a very convenient way to get around them.

"Where are we going?" she asked as Jon began to back down the driveway. "Wherever it is we won't see much of the countryside today."

"No," he agreed. "A roaring fire seems more appropriate than scenic dining, doesn't it? I thought we might eat on the way back, but I should have known it was likely to rain."

"It doesn't matter. Food is food."

Jon groaned, and rolled his eyes up in mock horror. "Food is *not* food, Delaney. Food is an experience. Or it should be."

Jessica laughed. "Try telling that to Nick," she advised him. "*He* thinks food is something you process."

"Yes, but according to you Nick has been surviving on omelets, chilli, spaghetti and Kentucky Fried since your parents left."

"I suppose *you* could do better," she taunted.

"As a matter of fact, I could. Care to try me?"

Yes, thought Jessica unguardedly. I think I would. Then she remembered he was talking about food and, infuriatingly, she blushed.

Jon, waiting for an answer, glanced at her and saw the pink tinge lighting up her cheeks, so that when she looked up from under her dark lashes, hoping he hadn't noticed, she was mortified to see a broad grin splitting his face.

"Well?" he asked, smoky eyes gleaming.

"I—er——" She swallowed. "Try what?"

"My chicken Kiev, of course," he replied with a very straight face.

Jessica swallowed again. "You mean tonight? At your place?"

"It's not Bluebeard's Castle," he pointed out. "Yes, Delaney. Tonight. At my place." The gray eyes glittered a challenge.

"All right." Jessica took a deep breath. "I'll risk it."

Jon's mouth twisted. "You make it sound as though I've invited you to be the main course instead of the guest of honor," he observed dryly. "Don't worry. My chicken isn't made from luscious..." He hesitated. "Virgins."

I am *not* going to blush again, Jessica told herself firmly.

She was so busy concentrating on keeping her cheeks promisingly pale and her eyes coolly indifferent that they were already parking beside the venerable brick house where Jon lived before she had managed to sort out whether it was being called "luscious" or being called "virginal" that discomfited her the more.

Jon's home was at the top of a steep hill only a few minutes' walk from the business section of old Port Arthur. It wasn't a large house, but somehow the mellow red brick and the tall tamarack growing by the door con-

veyed an impression of age and permanence. As though
it would always be there, immovable and reliable—like
its owner.

"Oh!" exclaimed Jessica, as Jon put his hand on the
small of her back and ushered her through the door into
a small hallway from which she could see into a light
and spacious living room. "It's very...modern, isn't it?
Very male."

"I sincerely hope so," said Jon, with a quiver in his
voice. "And no, Delaney, you may *not* come over to
redecorate for me. I have an intense aversion to frilly
lamp shades, fringes, ruffles and anything made of net
or lace."

"So have I," admitted Jessica. "On the other hand I
don't have *quite* the passion for black leather that you
have."

"Pity," remarked Jon, his eyes glinting at her. Then,
as she glared up at him, he moved behind her, looped
an arm over her shoulder, and led her toward the nearest
of his four well-padded leather sofas.

"No passion, I promise," he assured her, pushing her
down into the supple, enfolding softness of his favorite
material. "You haven't been here before, have you?"

"No." Jessica was trying to speak calmly instead of
like a frog with the hiccups, but the feel of his arm
around her and that muscular body pressed casually
against her side and murmuring about passion seemed
to have had a peculiar effect on her voice box.

"I thought not," he was continuing, apparently unaware of her predicament. "You can sit there and admire
the view, then—with suitable appreciation, I hope—while
I mix you a drink and do something about that fire I
promised to build you."

Jessica nodded, still not trusting her voice, and while
Jon disappeared into the kitchen she fastened her eyes

dutifully on the view. She had seen it a million times before from different angles, but it never quite lost the power to entrance her and to remind her that she was glad she had grown up in Thunder Bay.

In front of her the rocky formation of the Sleeping Giant reclined at ease in the unpredictable waters of Lake Superior. Even through the drizzle the Giant looked impressive, in lordly command of his bay. Jessica smiled at her own fancy, and let her eyes drift languidly over the gray panorama of the city, with the massive grain elevators towering close to the water, and in the distance the flattened protrusion of Mount McKay.

"Ah," said Jon's voice behind her, interrupting her moment of serenity. "I see you're doing as you're told for a change, Delaney."

"I'm admiring the view, if that's what you mean," replied Jessica, smiling slightly.

"Good girl. It's magnificent, isn't it?" He tugged gently at one of her trailing curls. "And it never fails to soothe my shattered nerves."

"Are your nerves often shattered?" she asked, interested.

"Frequently, when I'm around you. Here's your drink." He handed her a glass of something red and steaming.

Jessica decided to ignore the provocation, and fixed it with a doubtful eye. "What is it?"

"Mulled wine. Good for what ails you."

"Nothing ails me at the moment," she assured him, glancing curiously around the room. "You do very well for yourself, don't you, Jon?" She waved an arm that took in the view, the expensive furniture and the amethyst-streaked stone fireplace before which he was now kneeling with a lighted match.

"I do my best."

The match flickered and then flared to a bright orange flame as it took hold of the kindling in the fireplace.

Jessica lay back on the sofa, feeling warm and voluptuous, sipping the mulled wine and watching the fire cast shadows over Jon's scarred and striking face. Now, dressed all in black, he reminded her not so much of a lion as of some dark, pantherlike creature of the night. His back was arched toward the fire, one sinewy forearm flexing the poker, and the firelight was catching his hair and making it glow.

Jessica wanted to reach out to touch it, to curl her fingers in the deep golden waves on his neck, and she put down her glass to lean forward.

But at that moment he discarded the poker, uncurled his body, and stood up.

"That should do it," he began. Then he saw Jessica half crouched on the black sofa with her arm outstretched toward him.

"Going somewhere?" he asked softly.

"No, of course not." She lifted her hand hastily and made a quick swipe at her hair.

Jon smiled the smile of a cat who had a succulent mouse lined up for dinner, picked up his wine, and lowered himself down beside her.

"To new beginnings," he said huskily, extending his arm along the back of the sofa and raising his glass.

"Beginnings of what?" asked Jessica, bending her head to her glass so that she needn't look at him.

"Time will tell, won't it?" he replied enigmatically.

She raised her eyes quickly. There was a silken, almost dangerous edge to his voice that hadn't been there before. It frightened her—and at the same time she felt a tingling shiver of anticipation.

He was leaning forward now, his fingers in the long yellow curls down her back. Then he shifted his powerful thighs along the leather so that she could feel his wine-warm breath on her cheek.

"Jon," she gasped, panic-stricken for no reason. "Jon...shouldn't we eat?"

His eyes were hooded when he answered, and the deep baritone voice was not soft any longer, only cool.

"Ah, yes. Food. I promised you an experience, didn't I?"

"Yes," said Jessica in a small voice, wondering what sort of experience he had in mind.

"Right." He stood up abruptly, once again reminding her of a prowling cat. "Chicken Kiev coming up. You stay here and improve your mind with one of my books—or think about what you'd like for dessert."

Jessica swiveled around to see if his face would tell her what he meant by afters, but he had already disappeared into the kitchen, and she could hear him humming a harsh little tune beneath his breath.

She stared doubtfully at the big bookshelf which almost covered one wall. Not too many books on accounting. Mostly classics, tales of adventure and a great many maps, journals and articles about canoeing, the outdoors, wilderness travel and how not to get yourself killed in Northern Ontario.

None of the books particularly grabbed her attention and, inevitably, her mind went back to Jon's "afters."

Did he mean what she thought he meant? And if he did, did it matter? He would never force her to do anything she didn't want to do, of that she was certain.

So what was the problem?

It was dark outside now. She couldn't see the Giant. And the giant in the kitchen was making efficient, if unnecessarily loud noises with pots and pans.

The problem? That was easy, wasn't it? Jon, who had always been the one to solve her doubts and difficulties—when she gave him the chance—who had protected her from all threats, real or imagined, had suddenly become a threat himself.

No, that wasn't quite true. He had somehow become a mouth-wateringly desirable man. And that frightened her. She wasn't sure *why* it frightened her. But it did.

Besides, she thought, fumbling in the far reaches of her mind for an answer that made some sort of sense, you *can't* want to get involved with Jon, Jessica my girl. He's still only sober old Jon Stuart, chartered accountant. Where was the adventure in that?

When Jon called her to join him a few minutes later she was still trying to figure out what adventure had to do with anything, and why she should be thinking of it in terms of jungle cats.

She soon found out that this particular cat was a very good cook.

"Carol should have kept you," she told him, savoring each tender and tasty mouthful. "This is delicious."

"Carol didn't have much choice in the end. But I'm glad you like it."

"I do. How could you possibly have got it ready so quickly?"

"Unlike some people I think ahead. I prepared it several weeks ago and froze it. All that was needed tonight was a bed of rice."

"And the salad." Jessica supposed the reference to people who didn't think ahead meant her, and added bitingly, "Are you always so depressingly organized, Jon?"

"Usually," said Jon, not betraying his irritation by a muscle. "Are you always so depressingly ungrateful?"

"I'm not ungrateful. I told you it was delicious."

"At the same time managing to imply that being organized is almost as big a bore as being chartered." He broke off a piece of bread and buttered it, his eyes, very still and neutral, holding hers disconcertingly across the table.

With an effort Jessica managed to look away, letting her gaze roam rapidly over the small dining alcove, taking in the teak sideboard and trolley. Just right for the space available. More organization!

"No," she denied reluctantly. "I'm not against organization. I just don't like being told I can't think ahead."

"Mm." Jon gave her a lingering, unrepentant smile. "In that case I take it back. I'm sure you can think ahead when you want to, dingbat. The fact that you frequently don't is part of your charm."

"If that's supposed to be an apology it doesn't impress me," she retorted.

"It wouldn't impress me either," he conceded, the smile softer now as his eyes encountered the sparks flying out of hers. He squared his shoulders. "All right, I apologize. Your prudence and foresight are beyond criticism—but if they *weren't* the fact that you're a dingbat would be part of your charm."

Jessica choked and gave up. "I'm almost beginning to see what those hostesses saw in you," she sighed, trying to hide the fact that she wanted to laugh.

"Are you? That's encouraging."

Jessica wasn't sure she wanted to encourage him, but at least he wasn't playing the disapproving judge any more, so she allowed herself the luxury of a smile.

"How's the mysterious Reverend Michael?" asked Jon, adroitly steering the subject into less controversial channels.

"Oh, he's not mysterious any more," replied Jessica, happily following his lead. "As a matter of fact I've just drowned him in a barrel of beer."

"A disgracefully frivolous end for a man of the cloth," Jon reproved her, gray eyes dancing. "Couldn't you have thought of a more...ecclesiastical end for him? Poor Reverend Michael."

"Oh, he enjoyed it," said Jessica blithely. "And next I'm going to polish off the Colonel."

Jon threw back his head and let out a roar of laughter. "I hope I'm never a character in one of your books," he told her when he'd recovered. "I suspect you have a dangerously criminal mind."

"I have not. I'm the soul of respectability," she huffed.

"Are you really?" Jon appeared to be having trouble controlling his voice.

"No," she admitted, unable to hide a grin. "Not if I can help it."

After that the tension which had gripped them both seemed to dissipate, and they finished their meal with a companionable lack of strain, talking over old escapades—mostly Jessica's—discussing their respective families, as well as Jon's outdoor expeditions and Jessica's years as a teacher.

By the time they had finished their coffee they seemed back on the old easy footing. If it hadn't been for the speculative look that occasionally appeared in Jon's eyes Jessica could almost have believed he had forgotten he'd ever kissed her.

"I'll clean up, shall I?" she suggested quickly, swallowing her last gulp of coffee. The speculative look was back, and she felt unaccountably nervous and in need of something to occupy her hands.

"No, you won't. I have a dishwasher. Come and sit down, Delaney."

Jessica was already standing as he came from behind the table to put his arm quite naturally around her waist. She tried not to stiffen. But if she didn't she had an odd feeling she might dissolve against him like melting snow, and *that*, she knew, would be a mistake.

He led her into the living room, a bit like a parent dragging a reluctant child off to the bath or bed. No, she corrected herself, hastily banishing the disturbing image from her mind and trying, unsuccessfully, to concentrate on staying cool and unperturbed. *Not* the bath. And definitely not the bed!

The fire was dying down now, but Jon soon had it going again. When the warm blaze turned the shadows amber he came to sit beside her, and Jessica asked him why he hadn't switched on the light.

"Because we don't need it."

She stared at him. He was leaning back against the leather arm of the sofa, and his face was lit with a warm, deep, golden glow.

"There's something I have to find out, Delaney," he said softly.

"What's that?" Jessica's voice was only a throaty whisper.

He moved closer, and cupped his hand gently around the back of her neck. "Something happened last weekend. I need to know if it was real, or just some fleeting illusion of the autumn mist."

"There was no mist," she murmured.

"No?" In the semi-darkness his eyes were no longer gray, but black, and the hand on her neck was moving over her shoulder, then down further to touch the curving mounds beneath her blouse.

Jessica turned to him then, her lips parted softly in welcome, and Jon made a sound she didn't recognize and pulled her into his arms.

CHAPTER FIVE

THIS time Jon's kiss was not slow and gentle. It was hard, demanding, and it drew a response from Jessica that would have knocked her off her feet if she'd been standing.

His arms tightened around her, his big hands circling her hips, twisting her against him as he leaned over and pinned her back against the cushions. Jessica gave a little murmur and curled her fingers into his hair, holding his head so that his lips stayed locked with hers, tasting and exploring, teasing her tongue, and sweet as honeyed wine.

She pushed her hands beneath his sweater, marveling at the way her body fitted his, and marveling too at his strength and at the hardness of the muscles beneath her palms.

Then Jon was loosening the buttons on her blouse and before she was even aware of it the blouse was on the floor as, almost reverently now, he reached up to touch her breasts. She gasped, instinctively her body arched, and immediately, devastatingly, his hands fell away. Without knowing she was doing it, Jessica murmured a protest.

Jon swore under his breath, swore again, and sat up.

She gazed up at him, her eyes deep pools of purple in the firelight. "Jon?" she whispered. "Jon, what is it?"

"Here, put this back on," he said roughly, bending to pick up the blouse and practically throwing it at her.

Still trembling from the fire in her blood which had been lit but not put out, she took it and did as he said.

He had moved away from her now, and was sitting at the opposite end of the sofa with his elbows on his knees and his head buried deep in his hands.

"What is it?" she repeated.

"Why?" His voice was a strangled groan. "Why you, Delaney?"

"I don't understand."

"Don't you? No, you wouldn't would you? After all, as you informed me once before, I'm not the only man who's ever kissed you."

Jessica's violet eyes narrowed as she pushed herself up very straight. "What do you mean, Jon?"

"I'd have thought it was obvious. You're disappointed, aren't you? That that stimulating interlude we just enjoyed didn't go any further." He stood suddenly, casting gigantic shadows in the firelight as he loped across to the window.

"I was," she admitted, with tight-lipped honesty. "But now I'm not so sure. And if you mean what I think you mean, Jon Stuart, then you're even more of a pig than I thought."

She saw his shoulders stiffen, but his back was to her and she couldn't see the expression in his eyes. "I didn't know you still thought I was a pig," he answered bleakly.

He didn't sound angry. Only tired. Something in Jessica's chest seemed to break then, and she said quietly, "I didn't. Not until now."

Jon swung around at that and came to stand over her, his hands deep in the pockets of his jeans.

"I'm sorry," he said gruffly. "I had no right to take my own frustrations out on you. I *didn't* mean what you think I meant. I know you have your principles, and I respect that..."

Yes, thought Jessica, with a sense of horrified wonder. I had. But now it seems they weren't principles after all. Because if Jon hadn't stopped when he did... Oh, Lord, what was happening to her? It had always been so easy to fend off Richard whenever he became too amorous. Did that mean that Jon——? She shut her eyes. It couldn't be. Dear heaven, what a hopeless mess...

"What's happened to us, Jon?" she asked drearily.

He stared down at her, his face dark with shadows in the firelight, and then he laughed, a harsh, self-deprecating laugh. "I'm damned if I know. But just in case you hadn't noticed I'm a man, Delaney. Although I didn't expect to find myself on the brink of rape. Believe it or not I had something much more civilized in mind."

"How dull," said Jessica, trying to lighten his bitterness, which somehow she knew was not really directed at her. When he didn't answer, she added, "It wouldn't have *been* rape, you know."

"No. I realize that." His voice was curt, and he went back to stand at the window.

For a while he was utterly still, the palms of his hands pressed hard against the sill and his head bent between his shoulders. Then he straightened and said almost coldly, but still with his back to her, "Would you *like* me to take you to bed, then, Delaney."

Jessica's eyes traveled over him, from the dull shine of his hair, down his big, broad back to the deliciously firm hips and thighs. And she thought with surprise, yes. Yes, I would. But, oh, Jon, not in the mood you're in now. You've always been so kind, so predictable— and now I don't even know you. If I let you make love to me it would only be to satisfy lust, to compensate for the loss of Carol, perhaps, and when it was over you'd be filled with such guilt and self-condemnation. At least,

I think you would. And then you'd take it out on me, and I'd feel used. Cheap. I couldn't bear that, Jon. Not with you...

She lowered her eyelids so he wouldn't see the moisture that shimmered there, gripped both her hands tightly together, and said as calmly as she could, before frustration and distress overwhelmed her, "No, Jon, I think I can survive without your services, thank you."

He spun around so quickly that she scarcely saw him move; he took one quick step forward, and raised his hand. Then slowly it fell against his thigh, and he stood immobile, the outline of his body a huge black shadow against the wall.

"I suppose I deserved that," he said, after a long, pulsating silence. "I apologize."

"It's all right. I didn't mean it the way it sounded. Nobody deserves anything," replied Jessica, passing a hand across her forehead. She scrambled to her feet and began to tuck her blouse back in her pants.

"Don't they? Perhaps you're right. Delaney...?"

"Yes?"

"Delaney, this isn't what I meant to happen." Jon turned his face to the darkened window, and his voice was raw, choked with some rigidly contained emotion.

"I've said it's all right," said Jessica. She couldn't bear this any longer, and suddenly she was desperate to get away, to escape from this man who was making her feel as if her chest had just been crushed in a vice. "Please, no more postmortems, Jon."

"All right. No more postmortems." He hesitated, signs of an inner struggle distorting his scarred profile. Then, when she had almost decided he didn't intend to say more, he turned, stepped forward, put his hands on her shoulders and said abruptly, "I'm leaving town until Wednesday. Have dinner with me when I come back."

Just like that. Jessica gaped at him. After all tonight's drama and near disaster he was asking her to go out again just as if nothing had happened. Well, almost as if nothing had happened.

She shook her head blindly. For now, maybe forever, the last thing she wanted was any further entanglement with Jon. It seemed to hurt too much. She just wanted to go home, have a warm bath, go to bed, and forget that he had ever happened.

"No," she said flatly. "Thank you for asking me, Jon, but I don't think that's a good idea."

"I didn't *ask* you. And why isn't it a good idea?"

"I—we know each other too well," she muttered hastily—because he was looking belligerent and she had to say something.

Immediately his hands dropped, and he said coldly, "I see. I'm still boring old Jon, then, am I?"

"'Boring old'..." Jessica rubbed her eyes. After this evening, how could he possibly think she thought of him as boring? She stared at him, then rubbed her eyes again. What did it matter? All that mattered now was that she get out of here—at once—and into that bath where she would only have to absorb warmth without thinking.

"If you say so," she agreed.

Jon scowled. There was no mistaking his frustration. She saw him reach for the cigarettes he'd stopped smoking years ago, and when he discovered their absence he swore.

"I'll give you boring," he growled at her. "Just give me a chance, and you'll find out exactly how boring I can be."

Jessica tightened her lips and stood up very straight. "Don't threaten me, Jon. Just take me home, will you?"

For a moment he didn't move. Then, with another muffled curse, he seized her jacket, flung it around her shoulders and, without bothering to find a coat for himself, grabbed her by the elbow and hurried her into the night.

He didn't say a word as they sped through the darkened streets. He didn't need to. She could feel his baffled exasperation in every violent twist of the wheel.

"Good night, Jessica," he said as he opened the door.

She paused, staring into a face gone uncharacteristically hard. A face that had always been gentle when it looked at her.

Jessica. He had called her Jessica. She had a momentary qualm. But really she was too drained and bone weary to think about anything anymore. If something—or someone—needed worrying about, it would just have to wait until morning.

As Jon swung himself back into the car, she heard him say very distinctly, "Hell!" before the dark shape of his vehicle was swallowed up by the night.

Lying in the bath some minutes later, Jessica was also thinking, "Hell." This was supposed to have been a nice, relaxing bath which would wash away the traumas of the day. But it wasn't working out that way because, however hard she tried, she couldn't stop thinking about the way the evening had ended, remembering Jon's kisses—and his anger.

She had so hoped that everything would go back to normal after today. But it hadn't. In fact, everything was more confused than ever, and she felt bereft and disorientated, as if a part of her own body had been cut off. Not that she'd actually lost Jon, she reflected. But he was very angry. And she was afraid she had hurt him, even though he had showed more rage than hurt. She groaned, and ran a face cloth over her face for the third time. The truth was, he had hurt her too, by starting to make love to her, then drawing back, then acting like a

brooding black bear—except that she didn't suppose
bears brooded—and then coolly demanding that she go
out with him again just as if nothing had happened.

Her foot caught in the plug, displacing it, and half
the water disappeared down the drain. Jessica stared at
it grimly, feeling that at this moment she wouldn't entirely mind going with it, floating off into oblivion on
a gray tide. Instead, sighing heavily, she pulled herself
out of the bath and seized a towel.

In the morning she would think about Jon. Maybe by
then her mind would be clearer, and she'd be able to
figure out whether, unthinkable as it seemed, he had only
been considering her as a convenient replacement for
Carol. If he had, he was obviously having trouble with
the fact that she was Roger's sister. And what if that
wasn't it at all? What if his feelings had changed subtly,
become deeper? She hung the towel carefully back on
its rail. Well, what if they had? Did it make any difference? That was all that really mattered.

She stubbed her toe on the laundry box, mumbled a
few choice words, and made her way groggily to bed.

The next day was Monday, the second of her two days
off, and, by the time she awoke at ten o'clock, Nick had
already left for school. She brushed the tangled hair out
of her eyes and blinked. Last night must have taken its
toll, because she hadn't even heard the Cyclone Spoiler
start up. No doubt the neighbors had, though, she
thought glumly. One would have to be a very sound
sleeper, or very dead, not to hear the reverberating roar
so beloved of Nick and his cronies.

Jessica pushed the covers back and sat on the edge of
the bed, wondering why her head felt so awful. She had
only had two glasses of mulled wine last night. Jon, she
remembered, had downed considerably more, rather
purposefully, and with no visible effect at all.

Jon. Of course. *He* was the cause of her headache. She reached for the blue robe lying on the end of the bed, and decided she had some serious thinking to do about Jon Stuart.

But just as she reached the kitchen, having made a decision to put off all conscious thought until she had consumed several cups of bracing coffee, the phone rang.

Muttering under her breath, Jessica stumbled out into the hall to pick it up.

It was Richard, once again trying to convince her she had suddenly become the great love of his life. And on top of her headache, and her confusion over Jon, that was more than she could reasonably be asked to take just now.

"Go away," she said rudely. "Just leave me alone, Richard. I'm not interested."

When the phone rang again the moment she put it down, it was all she could do to stop herself from screaming.

But it wasn't Richard this time.

"Jessica!" Meg Delaney's voice trilled over the wires, and Jessica groaned softly.

This was all she needed. She had been desperate to talk to her mother all week, and now that she finally had the opportunity a very uncomfortable conversation would have to be conducted without benefit of morning coffee—or even of aspirin for her headache.

"Hello, Mother," she murmured.

"Jessica? What's the matter? You sound tired."

"I am a bit. I was out with Jon last night."

Oh, no! She hadn't *really* said that, had she? She clapped a hand to her forehead. What in the world had possessed her to encourage her mother's deluded ambitions?

"Mother, there's something I have to tell you," she began, before Meg could go off on some new tangent.

"I know, dear. Nick *already* told us, and of course your father and I are delighted. We've found some charming plates for you and Jon at this little shop in Kensington..."

"Mother, please——"

"And we'll see what we can pick up for you in Paris. We'll be heading over there next week. *So* looking forward to coming home and getting busy on the plans for your wedding..."

"Yes, but that's what I'm trying to tell you. There's not going to be a——"

"That's all right, dear, tell me another time; your father's just managed to get a taxi. He sends his love and you give ours to Nick, and to Roger too, of course, if he calls. And to Jon. Goodbye, dear. I'll call you next week."

"Mother!" Jessica's despairing cry was cut off by a loud click in her ear.

Oh, dear Lord! She leaned against the wall, covering her eyes with her hand. This mess was getting more impossible by the minute. It was bad enough that she and Jon had fallen out with each other, which they never would have been if she hadn't been fool enough to ask him to play that silly trick on Mr. Sanegra. But this business with her mother was getting out of hand. By now Jon must have explained things to his own mother, but Meg Delaney seemed determined not to listen to anything her daughter said. No wonder Nick hadn't managed to get a word in.

Wearily Jessica dragged herself away from the wall and almost staggered back into the kitchen. Coffee. She must have coffee. Maybe she'd be able to think straight after an overdose of caffeine.

Half an hour later she was slumped at the kitchen table holding her head in one hand and her fourth cup of coffee in the other. What *was* she going to do?

About what? asked a small voice in her head.

About Jon, of course. And about Mother's infuriating refusal to listen.

Well, Jessica, she answered herself, there's not a whole lot you can do about your parents, except hope they don't bankrupt themselves buying wedding presents that won't be needed.

Right, said the small voice. And what about Jon?

Jessica took a long gulp of coffee, drained the cup, and stared gloomily at the gray-tinged autumn sky. It was no good, there was no getting away from it. Whether she liked it or not, the time had come to face up to the fact that what she felt for Jon was much more than the old familiar affection. She wasn't even sure when the change had come about, but now, in the clear light of day, she knew she wanted him in a way she had never wanted Richard. She had felt nothing, not even a flicker of regret, when her ex-almost-fiancé had phoned.

Sighing, she ran her finger over a spot of grease on the table. She would miss her casual friendship with Jon. Sometimes it was still there, of course, when he teased her and laughed with her as he always had, but it was no use pretending they could turn the clock back.

Her eyes fell on the clock on the wall, and she frowned. Yes, the old relationship was over all right, and Jon, who had always been her friend, might some time in the future become her lover. She was wary of possible lovers, remembering still how deeply Richard had hurt her. But at least she could trust Jon, as she had not been able to trust that other, faithless man. Only... She closed her eyes for a moment. Only, he didn't seem able to trust himself somehow. Not with her. Because in his mind she was still little Delaney? Was that why he had become so harsh and unpredictable?

Jessica glared into her empty cup, reflecting that he had *wanted* to take her out again, and that she had told him they knew each other too well, letting him think she still thought he was stuffy and dull. But she had been so tired, so emotionally and physically drained—and deep down so furious with him for refusing to assuage the hungers he had aroused—that just then his feelings hadn't seemed to matter.

But now it was morning, and they did matter. They mattered terribly. Because he was Jon, and she couldn't bear it if they didn't stay... friends? She picked up the coffeepot and, discovering it was empty, slammed it back down on the counter.

All right, so what should she do now? Knowing Jon, probably she ought to stay out of his way for a couple of days, and then do what she could to repair whatever damage she had done.

Yes, that was what she should do.

Pleased that she had made a decision, but still unaccountably depressed, she jumped up and plugged in the toaster—along with the coffee machine.

"Brr. It's cold." Jessica shook her wind-blown hair from her eyes as she hurried into the house three days later.

"Not really," replied a voice from the depths of the living room. "You wouldn't be cold if you had the sense to wear gloves and boots and a hat, like everyone else."

"Good grief," she muttered. "You'll make someone a wonderful mother one day, Nick... When you grow up."

She stopped abruptly—because the figure lounging up to the open doorway wasn't Nick.

It was Richard.

"What are *you* doing here?" she gasped. "How did you get in?"

"Nick let me in before he left with his friends. He didn't seem very pleased to see me, either." The nose which Jon had described as elegant turned up in bored disdain.

"I don't suppose he was," said Jessica slowly. "He never pretended to like you much, did he?"

"No. The feeling was mutual."

Jessica stared at him, unable to believe that, after all the heartbreak this man had put her through, looking at him now she felt nothing.

"Richard, why are you here?" she asked, her voice not quite steady.

"Hang up your coat and I'll tell you."

"Why?" she asked suspiciously.

"Why hang up your coat? Because I want to talk to you, of course."

Jessica bit her lip. That sounded ominous. Whenever Richard looked at her with that dark-eyed, deliberately beguiling twinkle, and said in those deeply sincere tones that he wanted to talk to her, it invariably meant he wanted something. Usually something she didn't want to give. But he was here now, and she could hardly throw him out bodily...

Reluctantly she hung up her coat and followed him into the room.

"What do you want, Richard?" she asked baldly, surprised to find that even his physical presence was having no effect on her at all. In the old days her heart would have been spinning like a top—as it had that terrible day when she had bidden him her final goodbye.

Even now, feeling nothing for him, she remembered that scene in all its agonizing detail. How he had shrugged indifferently and told her she expected too much. And how she had looked at him, her heart in her eyes, pleading for some sign that he really cared.

But he hadn't cared. And now he was here, gesturing impatiently at her parents' sofa. "Come and sit beside me," he ordered.

"No, thanks, I'll stand."

"As you wish." He shrugged in that way she remembered. "Jessica, I'm sorry about Marie and Linda——"

"And Ilona," she interrupted. "Yes, you already said you were sorry. You always are—afterward."

"But Jess, dear, I really *am* sorry this time." He spread his arms wide, and switched on an impossibly engaging smile. "I've missed you."

"Really. Has Ilona given up on you, then?"

"Don't be cynical. It's not like you."

"Oh, yes, it is. I've learned to be cynical since meeting you."

"Jessica! You don't mean that."

"Oh, yes, I do."

He took a short step toward her, so that she could feel his breath on her cheek. He was wearing too much cologne as usual.

"My dear! All these months while we've been apart I've thought of nothing but how much I'd lost——"

"Ah," said Jessica, beginning to see where this was leading. "So Ilona *has* thrown you over. And I'm still the one who got away, aren't I? So you thought that after almost six months without seeing you I might be ready to change my mind—about filling that vacant spot in your bed."

Richard's mouth tightened, and she felt a faint flicker of apprehension. He had always had a quick temper, and he didn't take kindly to comments that assaulted his ego. She probably should have kept her mouth shut.

"I'm not particular," he told her now, the eyes which she had once thought so enchanting fixed on her with narrow speculation. "The sofa will do."

"Richard!"

"Don't sound so shocked, little puritan. Nick took great pleasure in telling me that you've been going out with Jon Stuart. You can't tell me *he* hasn't managed to get you as far as the sofa..."

Jessica saw the dark flush mottling his face, and took a hasty step backward. "Richard, I think you'd better go. Our last parting wasn't very pleasant, but at least it was civilized, and I *did* mean what I said. I wish you luck, but not with me. And I'm not about to change my mind."

He was breathing rather fast now, and she knew she'd handled things badly, so she said on a more placating note, "Please, Richard. You really will have to go. But I'd like us to part friends if we can."

That proved the wrong thing to say, too, because his mouth split in a thin-lipped sneer, and in one stride he was standing in front of her with his arms pinned tight around her waist.

"All right," he taunted. "All right, Jessica. Be friendly then. Kiss me. The way you used to."

Jessica ran her tongue across her lips, and Richard's eyes darkened. "I said kiss me." One long-fingered hand began to massage her bottom, and she gasped.

"If I do, will you leave me alone?"

"You won't want me to."

"But if I do?"

"If you want me to leave then—yes, I will."

She could see that he still had confidence in his power to seduce her. He had never really accepted that he hadn't succeeded before. In a way, feeling as she did about Jon, she could understand him now. It *was* hard to be deprived of something—or someone—you wanted badly. And Richard had a great many wants.

"All right," she agreed, taking a deep breath. "One kiss. But, I promise you, I won't change my mind."

"We'll see." Now both hands were stroking her bottom, pressing her against him, and with a little shudder Jessica lifted her lips and touched her mouth against his.

Immediately his grip hardened, and the pressure of his hands increased. His tongue started to force itself between her teeth—and Jessica started to struggle.

She didn't want this. Once, not so long ago, she had enjoyed his kisses. But not now. She had gone beyond that—beyond Richard—and she should never have agreed to this foolish bargain.

When she realized her struggles were only inflaming him further, she stood still—and in that moment the room became oddly silent. Then, as the pressure of Richard's lips relaxed slightly a deep voice murmured from outside the door. "Well, well, well. You don't waste any time, do you, Delaney? I trust you find your old boyfriend's embraces somewhat more—stimulating than mine?"

"Jon!" Jessica wrenched her lips away from Richard's, and leaped out of his suddenly slackened arms. "Jon, what are you doing here?"

"Witnessing a touching little reunion, it seems."

Richard took one look at Jon's large figure filling the doorway, and at the almost menacing look in his slate gray eyes, and mumbled something about leaving. "Unless you'd like me to stay," he added to Jessica, who was standing with both hands gripping the sofa behind her.

Well, at least he has that much guts, she thought tiredly. I wasn't a total idiot for thinking I loved him.

"No," she said woodenly. "I'd like you to go, Richard. Goodbye."

Richard straightened his rumpled shirt, gave her a careless smile, and walked toward the figure blocking his exit.

Jon, who was almost a head taller, stood looking down at him, not moving a muscle, a powerful and intimidating figure in the evening sun which streamed through the window.

Jessica held her breath as Jon pushed his sleeves slowly up his forearms, and then—after one heart-stopping moment—moved aside to let her tormentor pass.

The front door closed quietly, and Jon turned back to confront her.

"I have a strong urge to shake you till your teeth rattle," he remarked conversationally. "But I don't suppose I have that right."

"No," said Jessica. "You haven't." Then, thinking back to those rare occasions in her childhood when she had tried him to the point of retaliation, she added unwisely, "Not that that ever stopped you before."

"Don't tempt me."

Jessica decided discretion was the better part of valor. "Jon, what you just saw—it wasn't what you thought..."

"No? And what did I think?"

"Well, that Richard and I—that we're—well, back together or something."

"Now why would I think that?" He shoved his hands in his pockets and lounged back against the doorframe, his features registering only mildly bored indifference.

"Because—because we seemed to be kissing."

"Seemed to be?" He raised two dark, derisive eyebrows. "If that kiss was an illusion, then spare me a glimpse of the reality."

"That's not what I mean, and you know it." Jessica was beginning to resent his gibing mockery. "And, in any case, it's none of your business."

"In that case you don't owe me an explanation, do you?"

"No, I *don't*." She paused, remembering that in fact she wanted to explain to him, because she didn't want him thinking she was involved with Richard. "All the same, I wasn't kissing him," she muttered, less belligerently. "At least, I suppose I was in a way, but he made me."

"You're slipping my dear," Jon replied dryly. "You used to tell much better stories than that."

"But it's true..."

"Don't lie to me, Jessica." Jon straightened, and in two strides he was across the room with his fingers gripping her shoulders. "When I arrived on the scene you were lifting your pretty lips to his like a willing slave, and his hands were where I'd like to put mine at the moment—but not nearly so gently."

Jessica glared up at his sternly inflexible face in which only the eyes seemed to move. "All right," she said, through barely parted teeth. "All right, Jon. Believe what you like. I *don't* have to explain to you—and whom I choose to kiss *is* my own business. So please take your hands off my shoulders."

"Why? Don't you choose to kiss *me*?" His hard jaw hovered dangerously close to her lips.

"No," she bit out, her senses reeling from his closeness and from his obvious and unmerited contempt. "No, Jon, I do not want to kiss you. You're——"

"I know," he interrupted. "I'm too stuffy. Not to mention a bore."

"I didn't say——"

"Didn't you? Well, you certainly won't by the time I'm through with you, I promise."

As Jessica gaped at him his arms swept masterfully down her back, pulling her hard against him and sending waves of tingling longing up her spine. Then his fingers began to revolve, slowly, immediately below the waistband of her skirt, increasing the pressure until she gasped, and when she thought she was going to die of wanting him his mouth pressed down over hers, his tongue probing expertly, and calling forth a response from her that no amount of hurt or anger could restrain.

When she wrapped her arms around his neck, curved her body into his and let out an almost anguished moan Jon gave a short grunt of satisfaction, and held her away.

"Well? Were you bored?" he demanded, staring down at her upturned face with a caustic smile curling his lips.

Jessica swallowed. "No," she said. "Of course I wasn't. Jon, please stop playing judge and jury, and listen."

"Listen to more stories, Jessica?"

She thought about slapping that scornful look off his face, but decided that in his present mood he was all too capable of slapping back. "Oh, what's the use?" she muttered, twisting away from him. "You're determined to believe I wanted to kiss Richard——"

"How can I believe anything else? You're a very—responsive woman, as I've reason to know." One corner of his lip slanted crookedly. "But of course you're quite right. It's nothing to do with me, and I have no business behaving like a jealous lover. I apologize."

He didn't sound sorry, he sounded cool and in control, but, knowing him as she did, Jessica suspected the apology was sincere.

"It's okay," she said quietly. "I understand what it must have looked like, especially as I turned down your invitation the other day. The truth is, though, Richard promised he'd leave if I kissed him, and at the time it seemed the best way to get rid of him.''

"I see," said Jon.

"Don't you believe me?"

He shrugged. "I'm not sure. On the whole, I suppose I do."

"Then stop being so damned judgmental!" she exclaimed.

"And you stop calling me names, young lady."

Jessica's nerves, already strung to breaking point, snapped completely. "Stop it!" she shouted. "You're patronizing me again, Jon Stuart, and I won't stand for it. I won't be lorded over by an impossible, rude, judgmental, overbearing, bossy——"

"Bore?" suggested Jon helpfully, flicking her on the cheek in a gesture calculated to inflame her further.

It worked. "Out!" she yelled. "I've had it with you, Jon. Get out. Now!"

Jon smiled. "Certainly," he agreed, with infuriating amiability. "Don't stamp your feet too hard after I leave. It's rough on the flooring."

Whistling under his breath, he picked up the jacket he had left lying over a chair, slung it over his shoulder, and strolled unhurriedly in the direction of his car.

It was only with enormous difficulty that Jessica was able to prevent herself from sending her mother's favorite flower vase in hot pursuit. In the end she contented herself with a cushion, which hit the door just as he closed it, and landed with a disappointing thud.

Scowling, she walked across the room to pick it up. Then, clasping it to her breast as if to shield herself from further assaults on her emotions, she sank heavily onto the sofa.

"Oh, Lord," she groaned as indignation faded slowly into despair. "That's torn it."

She had wanted to put things right between herself and Jon, to repair the damage. Presumably that had been his intention, too, since there was no other explanation for his unexpected and ill-timed arrival. Only now things were infinitely worse, because he was half convinced she still had some feeling for Richard—who could blame him?—and was totally convinced that she was a frivolous and flighty young woman.

Jessica sighed, hugging the cushion closer. If only he hadn't been so damn superior she could have accepted his reproof without reacting. Because it was true she shouldn't have kissed Richard. That had been a big mistake, even if it wasn't strictly Jon's business. And, if only she hadn't lost her temper, they might have settled down to talk things out. To discover just what they were doing to each other—and why.

With a little moan of frustration she dropped the cushion on to her lap and buried her face in her hands.

She sat like that for a long time, but when, at last, she stood up there was a new look of determination in her eyes. Pursing her lips, she marched off to pick up the phone.

There was no answer, and the following day Jessica did some very sober thinking.

When the phone on his desk buzzed for the sixth time in fifteen minutes Jon swore under his breath and automatically extended an arm for the receiver. Then he listened for a moment to the soft, feminine voice murmuring at him over the wires and, with an incredible feeling that he had been in this space and at exactly this point in time before, he said, "No."

CHAPTER SIX

JESSICA heard the note of finality in Jon's voice, but in spite of it she knew she had to keep on trying.

"I've said I'm sorry I said those things about you. I do mean it, Jon."

"I'm sure you do. You're sorry your old port in a storm may not be there when you need it. And you're worried that next time you need a favor—someone to play your *father*, perhaps—I won't be there to oblige you."

"Jon!" cried Jessica, not quite believing that this harshly unfair judgment was being delivered by her long-time champion. "Jon, that's not true. Everything's happened so fast that we're bound to have made...mistakes. I've been thinking. Maybe we should try to start again from the beginning. Let things take their course——"

"Things *are* taking their course," he interrupted. "They took a definite turn for the worse last night. I've been thinking too, very seriously, and I've come to the conclusion that what happened between us must have been a brief burst of autumn fever before the reality of winter sets in. Two healthy bodies reacting with hormones instead of brains." There was a short silence before he went on relentlessly, "I'm not sure that you'll ever see me as a man with needs of his own, my dear, instead of some bossy boots who's there to keep you in line. You're a very charming young lady, Delaney, but the days when I was willing to alternate as a protector, a convenience and an authority figure are over. For good."

"Jon, that's not fair. I don't want a protector any-more. I know I do some crazy things sometimes, but that doesn't mean I'm a child, and I'm very well aware that you're a man with his own...needs. I *didn't* mean it when I said we'd known each other too long. It was just something to say because you insisted on an answer. And I was so tired——"

"Something to say?" He sounded impatient now, and at the same time mildly bored. "But the something you said was the truth, wasn't it? Oh, I know you're sorry now. Sorry because you think you hurt my feelings, I expect, and you're much too kindhearted not to feel bad about that. But don't worry, it'll take a lot more than a few home truths from you to damage my psyche irreparably."

"Jon, don't. You've got it all wrong..." Jessica was desperate now, knowing she was losing something precious.

"Have I? I don't think so." He paused. "As a matter of fact I'm sorry too, Delaney, and as I haven't taken this decision lightly I imagine it will be best if we don't see each other for a while. Eventually perhaps we can go back to being...good friends."

Friends? Eventually? For goodness' sake, didn't it matter to him...?

"It's because of Richard, isn't it?" she whispered.

He didn't answer at once, and when he did he sounded very tired. "No. Richard may have been the catalyst, but in fact it's because of a young lady who still throws tantrums and cushions—and a man who ought to know better."

"Better than what?"

"Than even to think about taking advantage of that impulsive child."

"I'm *not* a child! And it wouldn't be taking advantage——"

"It would. And I have a client waiting to see me, I'm afraid, so if you don't mind . . ."

"But I do mind!" She could picture him so clearly now, leaning back in his chair, fingers tapping impatiently on the desk as his eyes slanted over to the door. "Please, Jon——"

"No. I'm sorry. I'm going to hang up now, my dear."

She knew then that she had lost, but just before she put the phone back on its hook three barely audible words whispered at her over the line and she thought she heard him murmur very softly, "Goodbye, Delaney. Take care."

"Hi, Jess. Why so gloomy?" Nick looked up from his latest car magazine as his sister stomped into the living room, kicked off her shoes, and stared grimly at the grease on his shirt.

"I'm not gloomy."

"Yes, you are. You've been looking like a skinny drink of water for the past two weeks."

"I'm no skinnier than usual," retorted Jessica, eyeing the slender bones of her arms without much interest.

"No, but you're gloomier."

Jessica shrugged. "It's just the job, I expect. I'm not used to being at work so early, that's all."

"You've been doing it for three weeks," said Nick disbelievingly. "You must be used to it by now."

"Well, I guess I'm not. Why aren't you doing your homework?"

Nick, seeing the way the wind was blowing, picked up his magazine and beat a speedy retreat to his room.

Much more slowly Jessica followed him up the stairs and threw her bag listlessly on top of the bed. Then she crossed to her dresser, and began to study her face pensively in the mirror.

Nick was right. She did look gaunt. Her face had always been long, but now her cheeks were almost hollow and her eyes seemed sunk into her skull. Surely it wasn't possible to change so much in only two weeks? Because she had no doubt about when the deterioration had started. It had begun the moment she'd hung up the phone after that abortive call to Jon, and realized that not only had she lost an old friend, who could hardly be blamed for thinking she was still a little girl who saw him mainly as a rather sexy protector, but she had also lost…what? She wasn't sure, didn't want to think about it. But she knew there was an emptiness inside her that no amount of assumed lightheartedness could fill. Even Nick had seen that much.

She picked up a brush and began to pull it viciously through her hair. What was the matter with her? She didn't *love* Jon, after all. She had no desire to settle down to raise a family with him. The idea was ludicrous. And he had sounded positively bored with her that last time he had talked to her on the phone. Obviously she'd be well advised to forget all about the affair that hadn't happened. It was over. Jon didn't really care about her except in the way he always had, and now he was regretting his short-lived impulse to turn their friendship into something more.

The bristles of the brush scraped her ear, and she winced. Damn Jon Stuart! Even his behavior over Richard had probably been little more than brotherly overprotectiveness, coupled with a mildly bruised ego. So why was she allowing herself to lose weight over him?

She gave her reflection a thoroughly disapproving glare, followed by a bright, encouraging smile which she refused to admit made her look more like a jack-o'-lantern than a happy and carefree young woman.

"You're a fool, Jessica," she announced to the empty room. "And the sooner you stop thinking about that man the better." She brushed her curling locks into a rippling sheet of crackling, static gold, and wondered why this bracing conclusion only made her want to cry.

"There's no excuse for it," she continued to her hollow-eyed reflection. "Your job's going well, your book's going well—rural Ontario is positively littered with corpses—and with any luck you'll eventually manage to persuade Mother to stop solving Europe's debt problems single-handed."

Meg Delaney remained unconvinced that her daughter wasn't going to marry Jon Stuart, but Jessica had come to the resigned realization that there was nothing she could do about her parent.

She smeared cream carefully over her cheeks, and then added a discreet layer of makeup. Yes, that was better. And there was to be no more of this ridiculous moping.

Nodding to herself with more conviction than she felt, she squared her thin shoulders and marched down the stairs with her chin tilted determinedly—and, just as she reached the hallway, almost as if providence had been waiting, the phone rang.

Unable to squelch a sudden blossoming of hope, she tripped over her blue slippers and grabbed it.

It wasn't Jon, though. It was Brenda, asking her if she wanted to come to a party on Saturday night.

"It's a housewarming," she explained. "To celebrate the move to our new house."

"Oh," said Jessica. "Thank you. Congratulations on the new house, but I don't think..."

No, you don't, Jessica. She stopped herself just in time. Maybe you don't feel like going, but you made a vow to stop moping, remember? Maybe this party will be exactly the shot in the arm you need.

"Thank you," she finished quickly. "I'll be there."

She almost wasn't, though, because, not for the first time, the moment she tried to start her car on the night of the party it coughed and died.

"You need a new battery," remarked Nick, who was working on his Cyclone Spoiler by the light of a powerful flashlight.

"I know," Jessica bit back an urge to point out that he had a genius for stating the obvious, and instead gazed at him with as much forlorn sisterly charm as she could muster—with the result that he grudgingly agreed to drop her off at the party on his way to spend the night with a friend.

Forty minutes later the Spoiler swept around a corner like the cyclone it was named after, and came to a stop in a clearing on the shores of Lake Superior. On the way it narrowly missed several parked cars and a small knot of people making their way toward a brightly lit house perched high on the rocks above the water.

The moment Jessica's feet touched the ground Nick slammed the door after her, reversed rapidly, and swept back down the road in a shower of flying dirt and gravel.

"Did you enjoy that little joyride?" inquired a deep, smooth voice from behind her. "That brother of yours is going to kill himself one of these days if he doesn't stop driving his car like a misguided missile."

The skirts of Jessica's mauve dress swirled beneath her short wool jacket as she whirled around—to find herself looking into gray eyes that were as smooth and level as the voice. They stared at each other for one long, timeless moment, and then Jon took a slow step toward her.

Now he was standing very close, staring down, and his closeness, and the curious penetration of his gaze began to do strange things to her mind. Her body wanted to move even closer, to fling her arms around him and feel again the heady strength of his embrace. But her mind kept telling her to run away.

"Nick's all right," she answered him, holding her ground and keeping her eyes firmly fixed on the lake. "It's true he doesn't have much respect for his own safety, but he has enormous respect for his car."

"I'll take your word for it," replied Jon, not sounding as though he took it all.

As Jessica lifted her head, intending to tell him there was no need to be patronizing again, she saw his eyes wander over her with a peculiar blankness, almost as if he were looking at someone who wasn't there. Then he smiled without much warmth, ran a finger with surprising softness down her nose, and strode away.

She watched disbelievingly as his tall figure in tailored gray pants and a dark blue shirt disappeared up a short flight of steps leading to a long, low house made of cedar and Precambrian granite. The copper chimney and the eaves troughs glowed burnt orange in the light coming from a lamp over the water, and for a moment Jon's hair was touched with fire. Then he disappeared into the house.

Unaware that she was no longer alone, Jessica gave a long, despairing sigh.

"Hey, it's not that bad, is it?" asked a familiar voice beside her.

She looked up, startled out of her immobility.

"Richard!" she gasped. "Not you too. Brenda never said—— "

"Didn't she? Is my presence such a disaster?"

Jessica closed her eyes. Yes, it was a disaster. Not because it could possibly make any difference to the way Jon felt about her. He had already made it quite clear that he had no intention of resuming whatever it was they had started. But she didn't want Richard here, perhaps importuning her again, his very presence only serving to confirm Jon's conviction that she didn't know her own mind. Besides, she didn't even like Richard now. Not after their last meeting. His presence could only put a damper on an evening that promised to be quite damp enough as it was.

But there was no point in saying so.

"No," she replied, smiling with cool indifference. "Why should it be a disaster? Shall we go in?"

He had already fallen into step beside her, and there was nothing she could do except smile.

"I'm sorry about what happened, Jess," he began. "I didn't mean to come on quite so strong. It's just that you mean so much to me, and I guess I was—well, disappointed that you wouldn't have me."

"Mm. And surprised," remarked Jessica dryly, recognizing the signs that Richard's seduction routine was about to swing into high gear. She decided to nip it smartly in the bud. "I gather Ilona won't take you back."

"Jess, you're maligning me!" he exclaimed, his beguiling smile slightly more strained, but still in place.

"All right, let's forget it, shall we?" Her reply was curt, and at once the large double doors in front of them swung open to reveal Brenda, looking very pregnant as she smiled out into the crisp October night.

"Of course." Richard squeezed her arm, and Jessica flinched away.

"Hi, Brenda," she said brightly. Too brightly. "You have a beautiful house. How are you? How is——?"

Brenda, sensing the tension behind her friend's over-effusive smile, handed Richard over to Ben, and interrupted briskly, "I'm fine. Come and put your jacket in the bedroom."

Jessica kept her eyes on the polished hardwood floor, not wanting to see Jon among the crowd. She knew that sooner or later she would have to face him, but he had walked away from her outside, and she didn't want him to see the hurt in her eyes. She had never been much good at hiding her feelings, and she was afraid it showed. At the moment her pride seemed the safest thing to hang on to.

"What's Richard doing here?" she asked, as Brenda guided her into a bedroom piled high with coats. "You might have told me..."

"Oh, Jess, I'm sorry," cried Brenda. "I didn't know. Ben must have asked him. He's always doing things without telling me."

"Oh," said Jessica. "And the same with—with Jon Stuart, I suppose?"

Brenda glanced curiously at her friend's surprisingly pallid face. "Yes, that's right. But it doesn't matter, does it? You said you liked him."

"I did. I do. But we've had a—a falling out, I suppose you'd call it."

"No, I wouldn't. I'd call it a lovers' quarrel," replied Brenda cheerfully.

"I told you. We're not lovers."

"Too bad." Brenda decided to drop the subject. "Come on, let's go and join the gang."

A loud burst of noise came from the room with the raftered ceiling where the majority of the guests were gathered, and Brenda seized Jessica's arm and began to tow her toward it. Then, just as they reached the high arched entrance, the strains of some very loud dance music rose above the talk and laughter. Jessica hesitated, and, as she stood there, wishing she hadn't come and wondering where she could hide, an arm snaked around her waist from behind, and she found herself being dragged on to the crowded floor. Out of the corner of her eye she saw Brenda's eyes widen with concern.

"Dance with me, Jess," demanded Richard's voice, self-assured and, unbelievably, still confident of her acceptance.

Jessica opened her mouth to say no, but it was too late. They were already in the middle of the floor, hemmed in by eight or nine jostling couples, and at this point it seemed simpler to dance with him than argue.

What she hadn't bargained for was the fact that Richard had already consumed several drinks. The moment the music stopped he put both arms around her waist, pulled her up against him and kissed her, very thoroughly, and in full view of all the assembled guests— who immediately burst out clapping and laughing.

Only one person didn't laugh besides Jessica. As she struggled away from Richard's octopuslike embrace she saw Jon draped against the wall. There was a haggard look around his slate-colored eyes, and they were fixed on her with such repressed fury that she blanched. His expression frightened her. She had never seen a look like that on his handsome and beloved face before.

It was in that instant she knew for sure that he was indeed her beloved, that there could never be anyone else for her but Jon. There never had been. She had just been too blind to see that everything she had ever wanted had always been right there beneath her nose.

You're a fool, Jessica, she told herself, as the knowledge of her love twisted painfully deep in her chest. A deluded, idiotic little fool.

She wasn't sure what Jon was thinking as he watched her, but she knew with a flare of forlorn hope that the emotion she saw reflected in his eyes was not just that of an overprotective brother defending his sister's virtue, or even of a man who had been bested by another in the pursuit of a casual bedmate. The lines of his face were grooved, older. And that, she thought, half in hope and half in desperation, is the face of a man whose anger is barely held in, either because he can't bear to give up something he considers his by right, or because he has been deprived of something he greatly values. And Jon wasn't the possessive type, so maybe, please heaven . . .

She was afraid to finish the thought.

She was also afraid that if she moved toward him now there would be a scene of such proportions that it would totally disrupt this happy and lighthearted gathering. And she couldn't let that happen, could she? Not at her old friend Brenda's party.

But in the end she couldn't help it. She *had* to talk to Jon. Because she loved him. Richard's hands were still on her waist, but she brushed them away to take a quick step forward.

At once, as the music started again, Richard grabbed her and swung her back into his arms.

"What's wrong?" he asked. "You look as if you've seen a ghost. I hope it's mine. You used to like kissing me."

"That was a long time ago," Jessica snapped. "Please let me go."

By the time she was finally able to extricate herself from Richard's clutches she saw that Jon had his back to her. He had evidently just downed one stiff drink and was rapidly knocking back another.

Very tentatively she walked up behind him and touched his arm.

He swung around at once, and when he saw who it was his body stiffened and then relaxed again, just to the point where he looked like a spring that might snap to at any moment, whipping around anything that happened to stand in its path.

Jessica took an instinctive step backward. "Jon?" she said doubtfully. "Jon, what's the matter?"

He drew a deep breath, obviously fighting to keep himself under control. But in the end all he said, in that deep, level voice she loved so well, was, "Nothing that I'm aware of." He paused for a second, and then added with ill-concealed sarcasm, "I gather you're enjoying the party?"

"No," insisted Jessica. "I'm not. Jon, please..." She didn't finish the sentence because as she stood there, struggling for words, quite suddenly Richard, apparently made over bold by drink, came up and grabbed her from behind. She just had time to see the muscles of Jon's face tighten and one fist come up as if to knock Richard flat, before once again she was hauled out on to the dance floor.

She looked around desperately, praying that Jon would come to the rescue. But he didn't. Instead he lounged against the wall, watching her. And, she noticed with a jolt of optimism mixed with a terrible anxiety, he was still smoldering like a fuse that was lit to go off at any moment. As Richard's embrace locked her against him and the music rose to a wailing crescendo she couldn't suppress a flare of twisted gratitude to her old boy friend. He meant nothing to her now, but his actions had shown her beyond doubt that she loved Jon, and that Jon cared for her too—far more than he was yet willing to admit. Whether he loved her, she didn't know. But, oh, he wasn't indifferent. Not by any stretch of the imagination. She saw his fists clench, and recognized with a jab of fear that if she allowed Richard to keep on making advances to her any hopes of a reconciliation would be dashed. Jon, as she knew all too well, would only take so much.

She began to struggle in Richard's arms, but he only leered and tightened his hold.

"Please..." she whispered.

To her enormous relief, at that moment Ben, dispatched by an anxious Brenda, strode across the floor and demanded the right to cut in.

With very bad grace Richard released Jessica to his host's capable and nonthreatening arms.

"Thank you," she said. "Oh, thanks. Ben, I'm so—so confused..."

"I know," grunted Ben. "Sorry, I forgot about you and Richard, or I wouldn't have asked him. Is he being a pest?"

"Yes, but it's all right now. Don't worry, I'm fine."

She was fine, too, more or less, until Ben was distracted by a crisis about glasses at the bar, and was obliged to excuse himself hastily.

Jessica looked around for Jon, and saw that he was talking to a little brunette with light blue eyes. At least, the brunette was talking to him, and he appeared to be listening, although his eyes weren't on her. She was just trying to decide whether she ought to approach them when she caught sight of Richard weaving toward her again, wearing a hungry, and quite probably drunken smile.

She groaned, and looked around for a bolt-hole. There wasn't one, but the doors to the patio were ajar. She hurried toward them, dodging several entwined couples on the way. Just before she stepped outside she turned to make sure she had eluded Richard. Apparently she had—but Jon was now circling the floor, very slowly, with the little brunette in his arms. She was laughing up into his face, and Jessica tried not to look as the girl reached out both arms to link them intimately about his neck.

She hurried blindly through the door then, dashing away the mist in front of her eyes and wondering, in her distress, if Jon had felt the same when he'd seen her in Richard's arms.

She hoped he had.

A few minutes later she was shivering on the patio, her mauve wool dress no protection against the late October chill. She wrapped her arms around her chest and hugged herself, but it didn't help much. On the other hand, perhaps she needed the cold to clear her mind. Walking over to the granite wall surrounding the patio, she stared down at the dark, lapping waters of the lake which the Ojibway called Ketchegummee. A lake which bred rain and fog and storms to match the stormy confusion in her heart.

She wasn't confused over Jon anymore, though. She knew exactly how she felt about him. What she didn't know was how he felt about her. He had been displaying all the classic signs of a very satisfactory jealousy back there. But she wasn't sure... In the old days she would have known exactly what he was thinking. Not anymore.

She shivered, and listened to the waves hitting the rocks. What should she do now? Go back inside and confront Jon and his brunette? Or wait till he came to her? But he might not do that...

Her musings were cut off abruptly.

"Well, now," murmured a slurred voice in her ear, making her jump like a nervous cricket. "So this is where you've been hiding. Trying to play hard to get, Jess?"

Jessica swung around with a horrified gasp to find herself gazing at an obviously well-lubricated Richard, who was standing much too close to her and smiling with a slack-lipped but disturbingly meaningful leer.

She tried to back away, but the wall and the lake blocked escape. "Excuse me," she said firmly. "I'm going in now, Richard. It's cold."

"Ah, but I can warm you."

Jessica groaned silently. She'd walked into that one. "No, you can't," she informed him. "I told you it's over, Richard."

The slack lips twisted into an ugly line. "Why, Jessica? Because of that big adding machine in there? What can he give you that I can't?"

When Jessica didn't answer he put both hands on her shoulders and thrust his face up to hers. She struggled frantically to push him off, but his arms moved down her back and crushed her up against him, his lips searching for her mouth as her head twisted this way and that in a desperate effort to avoid him. "What's it like, Jess?" he jeered, his lips moving wetly against her ear. "Like taking candy kisses from your brother?"

Jessica made a sound that was a cross between a gasp and a cry for help, and, to her utter amazement, immediately Richard's body jerked backward.

"Why don't you ask that again?" suggested another voice, very conversationally and on a note that sent chills up Jessica's spine. "Perhaps I can supply you with an answer."

"Jon..." whispered Jessica.

But Jon wasn't looking at her. He had Richard by the scruff of the neck, and his lionlike head was hunched forward as slate eyes glared down into Richard's brown ones. His fist was only an inch from Richard's jaw.

"I—no offense," muttered Richard, who appeared to be mesmerized by that fist. "Just my little joke, you know. Jess and I are old friends..."

Jon continued to glare at him, not a muscle moving, and Richard relapsed into nervous silence.

"Oh for heaven's sake," growled Jon disgustedly. "You're not even worth hitting, are you? Get lost!" He spun Richard around, and shoved him forcefully in the direction of the house.

Jessica, too frozen now even to move, pressed her hands back against the wall and gazed doubtfully up at her rescuer. "Thank you," she murmured. "I think you came just in time."

"In time for what?" asked Jon, sarcastically. "After that hot little interlude on the dance floor I imagine you were warmed up nicely for a bit of fun. Have I spoiled it?"

"Fun?" echoed Jessica. "Jon, how could you?"

"Quite easily. Your friend with the roaming lips and the toothy smile appeared to be making excellent progress."

"And you weren't doing too badly either, were you?" she retorted with heat, responding to his tone automatically.

"What's that supposed to mean?" His voice, which had been cool and faintly taunting, suddenly seemed to hold a threat.

"Your brunette," she replied. "The pretty one, with the great big predatory eyes."

Jon didn't reply. Instead he glowered at her, his jaw thrust forward aggressively, and the light from the house glinting on his dark blond hair. More than ever he reminded Jessica of a lion.

When the crackling silence between them was stretched so tight that it was bound to snap at any moment, Jon said suddenly and peremptorily, "Fetch your coat. I'm taking you home."

"No, you're not," said Jessica at once. She might love him almost to desperation, but there was no way she intended to let him step back into his old role of law-maker and giver-of-orders. They were past that. But, contrarily, as she saw the muscles go rigid beneath his shirt, she wished she could put her hands on his shoulders to massage them and ease away his tension.

"I said get your coat," he repeated.

"Jon, I'm not leaving."

Instead of answering he took a quick stride forward, lifted his fist, and crashed it down on the wall, causing a small chip of granite to clatter on to the flagstones.

Jessica jumped, and at that moment the doors swung open and Ben hurried out on to the patio. "Hey, watch it," he warned. "Don't take out your troubles on my property. I don't see the point in being stuck with un-necessary repairs."

"Sorry," muttered Jon. Although he was partly in shadow now, Jessica couldn't miss the tautness of his jaw.

Ben laughed. "That's okay. Come on in and get warm."

Jon shook his head. "Thanks, but I'm taking Jessica home."

"No, you're..." began Jessica. Then she paused. What difference could it make? She didn't want to stay here, risking a further confrontation between Jon and Richard. And if she was ever going to have it out with this in-furiating man she had grown to love it might just as well be now as tomorrow. Given time to think, he might very well decide to shut her out again. And she couldn't bear that.

"All right," she said. "Thanks, Ben, I'll just get my jacket and find Brenda."

A few minutes later they were standing on the doorstep bidding goodbye to their hosts, and Ben, after giving Jon a very searching look, was asking half seriously, "Jon, if I let you drive Jessica home tonight, can I trust you not to toss her into the lake?"

"Don't count on it," replied Jon. "Come on, Jessica." He put his hand on the small of her back and began to propel her, none too gently, down the steps.

CHAPTER SEVEN

JON made no attempt to speak to her on the drive in to town, and after one look at his stormy profile Jessica was content to accept his silence.

When they came to a stop outside her house she looked up doubtfully as he leaned across to open her door. She was still furious with him for ordering her about as he had, but that didn't mean she intended to let him drop her off like a parcel. That *wasn't* why she had agreed to let him drive her home.

"Aren't you coming in?" she asked, swallowing a large mouthful of pride, and trying to sound cool and indifferent.

His face was very close to hers, and the dark blue shirt brushed enticingly at the bare skin just below her throat.

"You'd better believe I'm coming in," he responded tersely. "Though by the time I'm through with you you may wish I hadn't."

"You terrify me," she scoffed.

All the same, when she stole a glance at him as he walked up the path beside her with his hands rammed hard into his pockets, she did feel a faint twinge of alarm. He looked so fierce now, so completely unlike the Jon she knew.

He didn't say a word as he sank into the one unoccupied armchair in the living room, and watched as she threw a pile of magazines onto the floor and then sat down across from him on the sofa.

She gazed at him sprawled in the chair, one arm resting casually behind his head, yet with a hard, coiled tension about him that made her nervous.

When he remained silent, and continued to regard her with that grim, hard-eyed stare, Jessica finally took the bull by the horns and said quietly, "Jon, it has nothing to do with you under the circumstances, but I'd like you to know that Richard means nothing to me anymore. I'd also like you to know that I need a—a partner too, not a protector. If it took me too long to realize that, I'm sorry. I'm also sorry I lost my temper that day you found me with Richard——"

"Are you, now?"

She stared at him, eyes narrowing. He hadn't behaved any too well on that occasion either. And once more he was acting like judge and jury. But he was here, he had insisted on bringing her home, and—and he was on his feet, looming over her, looking about eight feet tall and very dangerous.

She gulped. "Yes, I am. Sorry. But if I did lose my temper it was your fault. You were so unbending, so damned critical..."

He arched his eyebrows. "It's a habit of mine, I'm afraid. I've never admired cheap little flirts."

Jessica leapt to her feet. "How dare you, Jon Stuart? I told you what happened, and you've no right to call me cheap. Or a flirt." Furiously she drew back a hand to slap his face.

He caught it easily. "No histrionics, please," he said, sounding bored.

Jessica's eyes beamed daggers of violet fury. "You," she began. "You..."

She stopped, because inadvertently Jon had pulled her forward, and just for a second her hip had brushed up against his thigh. The contact sent a spiral of flame through her body that had nothing to do with her anger, and when she gasped and glanced up at him she saw that something had happened to him too. His face was oddly blank, and he didn't seem to be sneering anymore.

She swallowed. What was the use of being angry? It was probably too late for that.

"All right," she said tiredly, pulling away from him to drop back on to the sofa. "*Don't* listen to me. Don't believe me. There really isn't anything more I can say."

She could say "I love you," of course, but somehow she didn't think that would help.

A change came over Jon's face then, a sort of weary skepticism that still gave nothing away. But after a long, uncomfortable silence he replied without visible emotion, "You could suggest that that scene on the dance floor didn't happen, I suppose. But I'm not sure I'd believe you. And I'm not much good at sharing my women, my dear."

"Oh, for heaven's sake!" exclaimed Jessica, exasperation once again overcoming despair. "Jon, couldn't you see that I didn't invite that business? It's not my fault that Richard turned into an amorous octopus the moment he had a few drinks."

"An amorous octopus?" Jon's gaze was still very skeptical, but his lips were no longer rigid. "Did you say...?" He stopped. "You always had a way with words, Delaney."

Jessica closed her eyes. He had called her Delaney again. When she opened them he was once more leaning back in the chair with both hands now linked behind his head . . . watching her.

"Jon," she said carefully. "I am *not* your woman. But if I were I promise you, you wouldn't have to share me with anyone."

"At least you've got that right," he drawled.

Jessica frowned. "Has this really all been about Richard?" she asked doubtfully. "Because if it has——"

"Not entirely," he interrupted. "It's also been about a madcap little girl I was very fond of, who somewhere along the line and without my knowing it turned into a very attractive woman."

"Oh," said Jessica, watching the way the muscles rippled beneath the tough skin of his forearms, and not sure how to answer that. "Er—thank you. I think. Does that mean——"

"I'm damned if I know what it means!"

"Oh," said Jessica again. "Well, I suppose I can't altogether blame you for that. I'm not a flirt, Jon, but it's true you've watched me pull some pretty dumb stunts over the years."

Jon raised his eyes to the ceiling. "Don't remind me," he muttered grimly. "And I apologize for calling you a flirt. I do know better."

"It's all right. As long as you didn't mean it. Jon...?"

"Mm-hm?"

"Do you believe me about Richard?"

"Oh, I believe you. As far as I know, and in spite of what I've said in the past, you've never lied to me, Delaney. Told me stories perhaps, but never lied."

"No," she agreed. "I haven't. Not seriously." Then, distracted, she asked, "What would you have done if I had?"

He smiled then, for the first time that evening, and it was that slow, sensuous smile that melted her bones. "Well," he began meditatively, "what I'd like to have done, you wouldn't have enjoyed one bit——"

"No," cut in Jessica hastily. "I don't suppose I would. But what I was trying to say—I mean—well, if it isn't

Richard, and if you could get over thinking I'm still a child..."

"But I haven't by any means got over that, Delaney." His lips twisted. "You don't make it easy."

Jessica felt her temper start to come to the boil again, and made a determined effort to control it. "All right, so you haven't got over it. But the fault's not all mine. You were a swine the last time I saw you, you were a swine when I talked to you on the phone, and tonight..."

"Tonight I outdid myself," he concluded dryly. "Yes, I know. I've been told that already. By Ben."

Jessica glared at him. "That's nothing to be proud of," she snapped.

"Mm. You may be right," he agreed, as his eyes fastened on her with a brooding speculation. "And I suppose you expect me to apologize again, don't you? For being a swine?"

"*Are* you apologizing?" Jessica asked, as his look made something warm and wonderful curl in the pit of her stomach.

His only answer was a grunt—and a crooked smile.

"Oh, well, it doesn't matter," sighed Jessica after a short silence. And then, following a much longer moment during which she felt as if she were drowning in the smoky intensity of his eyes, she admitted, "I suppose you had *some* provocation."

"You might say that."

"But so had I," she pointed out. "Why *have* you been so brutal lately, Jon?"

He leaned his head against the back of the chair, and stared pensively up at the ceiling. "I'm not sure I have," he murmured, "but *if* I concede that my behavior left something to be desired, I suppose it was because I'd decided I had better take your education in hand before someone else got you into serious trouble. But when I arrived to see to it your Richard already had that angle covered. Rather efficiently. Or so it seemed. And I didn't like it.''

"Didn't you?" said Jessica happily. "I'm so glad." As Jon lowered his eyes from the ceiling to turn them warningly in her direction, she added quickly, "Jon, what made you come in tonight? And why did you say I might regret it?"

"Ah," he said, leaning forward suddenly, and then rising to his feet with catlike speed. "This is why."

Before she knew what was happening he had dropped down onto the sofa beside her and was twisting his fingers in the hair at the back of her neck, forcing her to face him.

"Wh-what?" she croaked, her eyes wide on his face.

"This." Jon bent his head swiftly, crushing his lips against hers, the fingers in her hair tightening so that she couldn't move. Not that she wanted to, as his free hand circled slowly down her spine, playing a wild and glorious symphony on her nerve ends.

Jessica linked her own fingers in his waving hair, then moved them in an enchanting exploration of his neck, his shoulders, his broad back . . .''

Somehow she found herself lying back against the cushions, and now Jon's large hands were on her waist, and then sliding up to touch her breasts through the clinging material of her dress. His kiss was fierce, hungry, but as Jessica kissed him back she sensed that even now he was holding back.

She was right. Just when she thought she could bear this sweet torture no longer, he brushed a gentle kiss across her eyelids and sat up.

"And that's enough of that," he said, a little thickly. "Otherwise things may get out of hand."

"Does that matter?" asked Jessica.

"Yes."

"Oh." She hesitated. "But, Jon, I really *have* grown up. In fact, I feel as if in the past two weeks I've aged ten years."

"Good Lord, I hope not." Jon's eyes were still bright with passion, and he was breathing deeply as he ran his thumb abstractedly down her cheek.

"Well, five, anyway," she amended, smiling. "Is that old enough for you?"

"I'm damned if I know, Delaney, as I said before. I suppose it'll have to be. Provided you have no more Richards hidden away in the woodwork."

"Of course I haven't."

"That's good. Because it wasn't until tonight, when I saw you with Richard again, and wanted to rearrange his face for him and do even less gentlemanly things to you, that it occurred to me I might find life a little dull without my Delaney."

"So you decided to behave like a dictator," said Jessica with an edge to her voice.

He grinned without noticeable compunction. "I suppose I did."

"And now?" she asked, trying not to hold her breath.

Very slowly, and with great purpose, Jon put both arms around her shoulders and drew her against his chest.

"And now," he continued, with a sort of grim resignation, "I suppose I'll have to let things take their course. And hope I'm not moved to contemplate your untimely end too often."

"You can't murder me," murmured Jessica into his neck. "It's not..." She giggled. "It's not done to murder respectable schoolteachers. Which I was."

"Good grief!" exclaimed Jon. "How inhibiting."

Jessica lifted her head and batted her long eyelashes at him as she stroked her hand lightly along his thigh. "I don't believe you're ever inhibited," she said with studied provocation.

"Keep that up and I won't be," he growled, his eyes glinting. "You're asking for trouble, Delaney."

"I know," she said demurely. And then, her own eyes sparkling, "Am I going to get it?"

"Oh, indeed you are." The glitter deepened as he leaned toward her and pulled her roughly back into his arms.

"I like trouble," observed Jessica contentedly some time later when Jon, breathing raggedly, tore his lips from hers, and pushed her back against the arm of the sofa.

He groaned, "Don't I know it!"

He raised his hand and curved it firmly around the back of her neck, and Jessica heaved a happy sigh and ran her fingers tenderly over the jagged scar on his forehead.

"Jon," she began reluctantly, after a long pause. "There *is* something—someone..."

"Who's that? Not another octopus, I hope, because I won't stand for it."

"No," said Jessica, on a slight note of malice. "I was thinking of that clinging vine *you* had wrapped around you at the party."

"Ah. You mean my old friend Heather." He nodded, smiling nonchalantly.

"I guess I do." Jessica waited for an explanation that didn't come. "Jon Stuart," she said crossly, "you can't..." Then she saw that he was laughing at her, took a deep breath, and subsided, knowing she would get no further with him tonight. Not when he was in that intentionally aggravating mood.

She gave him a dirty look, and immediately his eyes glinted, and he started to reach for her. But, to her great disappointment, he changed his mind and stood up.

"You're not *going*?" she protested.

"Indeed I am. If I stay I may be guilty of seducing my old friend's sister right under the parental roof. Hardly an act of gratitude after all their kindness."

Jessica stared up at him, her eyes teasing, and her wide mouth turned down in a deliberate little-girl pout.

"I don't want you to go," she moaned aggrievedly. "And I think I'd like to be seduced."

"I don't doubt it," said Jon gruffly. "But I'm not going to be the one to do it."

"Why not?" she asked, sounding like a child deprived of a promised treat.

Jon shook his head. "Because you're Delaney," he replied flatly.

And Jessica knew that was all she was going to get out of him tonight. Shrugging resignedly, she gave up the Shirley Temple act, and grinned.

In another moment he was bending over her, his long arms on either side of her hips. She smelled the spicy, male warmth of him as his mouth touched her lips very lightly, then he brushed a long blond tendril off her forehead, straightened, and strode quickly across to the door.

"I'll call you tomorrow," he promised. "Behave yourself, Delaney."

She caught a glimpse of a streetlight from the hallway, and then Jon had vanished, like a very sexy phantom, into the night.

Some time later Jessica stood up, yawning. She felt restless, incomplete. But Jon would be back. He had said so. And one day, perhaps soon, he would still that restless turbulence for good.

Her face was wreathed in a soft, dreamy smile as she drifted up the stairs to her room.

The moon came out just then, and a pale light filtered through the window, casting soft, dreamy shadows to match her mood.

Yes, there were still shadows. She knew that.

She loved Jon, but he had only said that life would be dull without her—not that he loved her. It was impossible not to believe he wanted her, of course, but wanting and loving were not the same. And, because she was who she was, she couldn't even be sure that Jon, because he was who *he* was, would ever choose to satisfy those wants. Not if he thought he was taking advantage of a child who happened to be called Delaney.

Jessica sighed and began to pull off the soft mauve dress, as a cat howled somewhere in the night.

She supposed she *could* try to curb any wayward tendencies on her part to instigate anything he might consider troublesome or crazy—but dammit, she wanted Jon to fall in love with *her*! Not some mythical creation in his mind of the woman he thought she should be. She smiled wryly. The next few weeks could prove to be quite a challenge.

Pulling a clean nightgown over her head, and forgetting she had already laid one on the bed, she nodded with sudden determination, and gave a little hop before she jumped beneath the covers.

Two weeks later, though, as the once green-gold leaves began to drift crisply to the ground, she started to wonder if this particular challenge was going to prove insurmountable.

She saw Jon almost every day, and he was attentive and kind and teasing—and a bit dictatorial; in fact, he was the Jon she had always known, except that this Jon sometimes kissed her, with agonizingly chaste restraint. At least, she found it agonizing, because he never touched any part of her that might be considered private, and when he took her out it was invariably to some public place where passionate lovemaking in corners would be considered a disgraceful breach of good taste. He didn't take her to his home again, either, and when Jessica asked him why not, and began to run her hand suggestively along his thigh he shoved it away and answered almost angrily, "Because you're Delaney."

While in a way she respected his restraint, and accepted that this was his way of letting things take their course, Jessica found that every time she saw Jon now she wanted more of him than he was willing to let her have. Because she loved him she wanted all of him, but sometimes she despaired of ever getting past the wall of respectability he had built between them. She had even learned that he had finally told his mother they were not engaged. That hadn't done much for her morale either.

Then, one evening when she arrived home from work, Nick informed her that she had just missed a call from her fiancé.

"He's not my fiancé," said Jessica automatically.

"Oh, yeah? Tell that to Mother."

"But he's not."

"Well, if he's not he soon will be. Otherwise why has he been hanging around you like a fly in a butcher's shop all month?"

"What a charming comparison," observed Jessica, trying hard not to laugh.

"All right, like next door's Fido when the bitch down the road is in——"

"Nick!" Jessica held up her hands. "I get the picture."

She did, too, although a picture of Jon besieging her door all night and howling piteously, as next door's Fido was wont to do at certain seasons, did not entirely square with the actuality of Jon's quietly pervasive presence in her life.

"What did Jon want?" she asked now, noting that Nick was about to take refuge in his car without bothering to pass on any message.

"You, I expect," replied her brother, grinning salaciously.

Jessica decided he was growing up much too fast. "That's quite enough," she said in her most repressively schoolmarmish tones. "Now, tell me why he called. At once."

Nick, after one look at her face, said quickly, "Yes, *ma'am*. He said he wouldn't be over this evening, after all. Something's come up. But he wants to take you out to dinner tomorrow. Somewhere special, he said, and you're to wear something pretty. Hey!" He gave her a sly grin as a further idea occurred to him. "Maybe he's going to propose to you tomorrow, Jess. What do you think?"

"Don't be ridiculous," replied Jessica, wishing her face didn't feel quite so annoyingly hot.

Nick left the room, still grinning, and whistling an aggravating little tune under his breath.

Jessica contemplated throwing the nearest cushion at his head, but it was already smudged with some substance which looked as though it had come off a car, so she thought better of it, and went into the kitchen to make a sandwich. Nick was going over to his friend's again tonight, and if Jon wasn't going to be with her she didn't much feel like bothering with a meal.

Slapping a quantity of cucumber, tomato and lettuce between two hefty chunks of brown bread, she pulled out a plate, sat down, then changed her mind and carried the plate upstairs.

If she was going to be on her own tonight she might as well press on with her mystery. It had been sadly neglected of late.

She typed half a page, then stopped. Munching thoughtfully at her sandwich, she stared glumly at the paper, then shook her head and ripped it out again.

Half an hour later, after this process had been repeated three times, she gave up.

"To hell with it," she muttered, jumping restlessly to her feet. "I'm obviously not in a creative mood tonight. Besides, I'm hungry."

Jessica glanced doubtfully out of the window. It wasn't raining. Before long it would start to snow. But not tonight, and right now she didn't feel like sitting at home staring at blank sheets of paper. Her watch told her it was only eight o'clock. Plenty of time to grab a bite at Francillia's before coming home to catch an early night.

Slipping a coat over her black pants and sweater, she hurried outside to start her car.

Francillia's did not come under the classification of fine dining, but it was only a short drive from the house, and it served good, basic meals of the lasagne and spaghetti persuasion. She and Jon had often eaten there before taking in a movie or visiting friends. It featured red and white checked tablecloths and dim lighting, and tonight Jessica was grateful for the dimness as a waiter led her across the floor to a table for two in the corner. She was tired after her unsuccessful struggles at the typewriter, and the prospect of eating spaghetti under the full glare of fluorescent lighting held about as much appeal as being caught in front of a class of giggling children with a rip down the back of her pants. That had happened to her once, and it wasn't her favorite memory.

Then, as she began to take the seat the waiter was holding for her, Jessica stopped being grateful for the lack of illumination—because if she had been able to see from the door what her eyes were taking in now she would never have got as far as this corner.

In fact, she would never have entered the restaurant at all.

The waiter frowned impatiently as she stood in a frozen crouch above the seat. He cleared his throat, and she blinked and came to her senses. Standing up straight again, she informed him distractedly that she was sorry, but she wouldn't be eating here after all.

Then, just as she moved away from the table, preparing to make a bolt for it, the cause of her confusion looked up from his conversation and saw her.

"Delaney!" exclaimed Jon, in a voice which carried further than he'd intended. "Delaney, I didn't see you come in."

He was seated in a secluded corner with a female companion who was smiling up at him with an easy, unworried possessiveness.

"Obviously not," murmured Jessica in a small, choked voice, as she began to make her way to the door.

"What does *that*...? Oh, I see." He gestured at his companion, a glamorous young woman with a great deal of black hair piled in an unusual pompadour atop her attractive head. "Delaney, you've met Carol. Come and join us."

"Yes, I've met Carol." Her voice was very controlled. "And thank you, but I wouldn't dream of interrupting your little reunion. Now, if you'll excuse me..."

"Jessica! Stop!"

Heads began to turn in their direction as Jon's voice bellowed across the room, and suddenly Jessica's control snapped like wire that had been strung too tightly.

If only she could have got to the door it would have been all right, but, at the sound of that commanding voice, ordering her to come back when her heart was breaking, the last vestiges of her common sense deserted her.

In a flare of rage and disillusion so overpowering that she scarcely knew what she was doing, she marched across to Jon, picked up his wineglass and dumped its entire ruby red contents over his shining blond head.

Then she picked up Carol's glass, and a moment later its contents too were cascading in rivers over Jon's stunned and frozen face.

CHAPTER EIGHT

FOR a second there was dead silence in the restaurant as the patrons of Francillia's enjoyed the best free entertainment they'd had in years.

Then a low, excited hum rose up all around them, and the waiter took Jessica's arm very firmly and began to pull her quickly toward the exit. Seconds later she felt a tight grip on her other arm as reinforcements arrived and she was turned around and propelled speedily and efficiently through the door.

The last thing she saw as she looked back over her shoulder before being pushed outside was Jon's dark, furious face as he sat glaring after her, his body crouched forward like that of a lion about to attack, and with the red wine still gleaming wetly on his cheeks.

To Jessica it looked very much like blood.

She felt the eyes on her back as, after murmuring embarrassed apologies, she climbed into her car and turned the key.

The proprietors of Francillia's were making sure she left the premises, and were taking no chances on a repeat performance of this unexpected assault on their clientele.

It was not until almost two hours later, as she sat in the darkened kitchen of her parents' house staring blankly down at a ghostly white table, that it occurred to Jessica that she still hadn't eaten. Unless you counted that vegetable sandwich she had made when she'd come home from work. She sighed, a sad, very lonely sigh. Somehow she knew it would take much more than food to banish the hollow feeling in her stomach. A hollowness that was caused not so much by hunger as by the knowledge that more than wine had been spilled when she'd emptied those glasses over Jon's unsuspecting head.

All her dreams had spilled away too.

She saw again that look of astonished fury on his face, and her lips twisted painfully. She shouldn't have done it, but she couldn't really regret it, because for once her impulsiveness had paid off in a kind of bittersweet sense that this time justice had been done.

She tried to smile, but her eyes filled suddenly with tears. Justice? What did justice matter? Surely it was a pitifully poor substitute for love—for years that would pass too slowly as she grew more empty and bitter, and more alone...

"Oh, Jon," she whispered brokenly. "Jon, how could you?"

At last, as the hands of the clock touched midnight, very slowly she dragged herself to her feet. Life, she supposed, must go on. Even though the idea that she had a job to go to in the morning didn't seem quite real at the moment, she knew she had to hang on to the fact that, just because Jon had let her down, it didn't mean she had to stop breathing.

It's not even as if he did let you down, really, she added to herself with brutal honesty as, some time later, she lay sleepless on top of her rumpled, uninviting bed. He never made you any promises, Jessica.

No, he hadn't made her any promises. But he had lied. He had insisted that his affair with Carol was over when it obviously wasn't. If it had been over they wouldn't have been together, dining in intimate obscurity at Francillia's.

She gave a choked little sob, and thought again of Jon's face dripping crimson wine. Oh, yes, not being welcome at that restaurant any longer was a very small price to pay for—for what? Satisfaction, yes, but an utterly meaningless satisfaction.

She closed her eyes, willing herself to fall asleep. It didn't work, and when, not very much later, she heard the sound of fists thundering on the front door and Jon's angry voice shouting at her to open up this minute, it wasn't satisfaction she felt at all, but a kind of exhausted apprehension.

She had been through a lot these past few hours. An emotional scene with an aggressively angry Jon who had got no more than he deserved was more than she could take at—she glanced at her watch—two o'clock on a chilly autumn morning.

The pounding on the door didn't let up for a second and, amid a tumult of more pressing emotions, Jessica began to worry about her sleeping neighbors. They were remarkably tolerant of the mechanical noises emitted by Nick's car, but it was asking too much of them to expect an equal tolerance for this strident assault on her door in the small hours of the night. She would have preferred to have ignored Jon, but it was becoming increasingly obvious that he wasn't going to allow her that option.

Sighing, she swung her legs over the side of the bed, and pattered across to the window. A blast of cool air hit her face as she threw it wide and shouted above the hammering, "Jon! Be quiet. Go away."

"I will *not* go away. Open the door!"

"No."

"I said open the door!"

"Jon, shut up. You're disturbing the neighbors."

"To hell with the neighbors. And don't tell me to shut up."

"I wouldn't have to if you'd just..." She paused as a light flashed on next door, followed by another one across the street. "Jon, please be quiet."

For one brief instant he was absolutely still, poised with a fist above his head. Then, very slowly, he lowered it. "Jessica," he said in a hard, purposeful voice that carried upward like the prelude to the last trump, "Jessica, if you don't open this door I'm going to *break* it down. And that will make a hell of a lot more noise than I'm making now."

Jessica thought about that. Yes, it probably would, and it would also be difficult to explain a broken door to her parents.

She could threaten to call the police, of course, but in Jon's present mood she didn't think that would have much effect.

"I'm not dressed," she answered, in a last futile attempt to avert the inevitable.

"Good."

Jessica laughed emptily. In other circumstances she might have found that comment almost promising, but as it was now...

She shook her head, and reached for her blue robe. As it was now, there wasn't anything remotely promising about that tall, menacing figure glowering up at her through the darkness. At least, she supposed he was glowering, although all she could see was the outline of his impressive shoulders in the faint light from her neighbors' windows. She took a long breath, telling herself that, when it came right down to it, it was only Jon out there, and she had never been seriously afraid of Jon Stuart in her life.

No, intruded an inner voice she had been hearing too much from of late, and you've never dumped wine all

over him in your life either—even if he did deserve it—
or behaved like a jilted prima donna in public.

Ignoring the voice, she called out, "All right. Wait.
I'm coming."

"Good. Hurry up," came the uncompromising reply.

But just as Jessica reached the bottom of the stairs
the phone rang.

"Are you all right, Jessica?" whispered a querulous
voice from next door. "If that young man is causing you
any trouble..."

"It's all right, Mrs. Hujanen," said Jessica quickly.
"It's just an old friend of mine who's been trying to
wake me up."

And there go the last shreds of my reputation in *this*
neighborhood, she thought morosely, as she crossed the
hall to meet retribution in the form of her old protector.

She thought for a moment, as Jon strode across the
threshold and slammed the door, that retribution was
going to be instant and painful. From the way his big
hands curled at his thighs and his eyes flicked furiously
over her, she had a feeling that if she allowed him to get
too close to her the outcome would not be agreeable.

"Don't even think it," she told him, clasping her hands
tightly behind her, and backing away down the hall.

"If you don't have a damn good explanation for that
little scene, believe me, I'll do more than think it." His
jaw was solid granite, and he was advancing toward her
with a grim determination she didn't trust.

Jessica's precarious control slipped down a notch.
"Jon," she managed to grate out, "don't you think it's
you who owes *me* the explanation?"

"What?" For a moment she saw a faint frown of
doubt between his eyes. Then it was gone, and once more
he was glaring at her. "No, Jessica, I do *not*. There's
nothing to explain."

She stared at him. He had changed from the sport jacket he had been wearing in the restaurant into a dark gray rib-knit sweater, and his wavy blond hair was still slightly damp, but no longer stained bloodred with wine. Just for a second she wondered if Carol had been with him when he'd changed, and she scowled without knowing she was doing it. Then she had to bite off an explosion of appalled indignation at the supreme arrogance of this man who apparently thought it was perfectly all right to break a date with her so that he could entertain another woman. Yet even now, in the midst of her hurt and anger, and with hot tears pricking at her eyelids, she found she had to grip her hands together to prevent herself from reaching out to touch him. He looked so—so male and aggressive, and, in spite of everything, so heartbreakingly desirable...

For just an instant desire flared more brightly than ever as Jon took her by the arm and propelled her swiftly ahead of him across the hall. Then it was extinguished by a wave of resentment.

As soon as they entered the living room he switched on the light and swung her around to face him.

"Now," he said harshly, "*what* was that all about?"

Jessica gaped at him. "Don't you *know*?" she asked. Her eyes, which had been luminous and bemused, turned bright with outrage as her sense of betrayal grew and threatened to choke her.

"Should I know?" His voice was hard, unyielding.

She couldn't believe it. He was behaving as if *he* was the injured party, when it was patently obvious he had been deliberately deceiving her all along. She'd been so easy to deceive, too, she reflected bleakly. Because she'd trusted him. That was what hurt the most. That Jon, of all the men in the world, should be the one to betray her—just as Richard had done.

But Richard didn't matter. Jon, who was standing with his hands on his hips now, like a general about to order his troops into battle—he did matter. And yet he seemed completely unaware of what he'd done.

Something snapped then. Jessica could contain her pain and grief no longer, as for the second time that night all reason and control flew out the window.

"How dare you?" she almost spat at him. "How *dare* you pretend you don't know why I'm angry? Dammit, you had a date with *me* tonight, Jon. And you broke it so you could go out with another woman. And not just any woman, oh, no! You told Nick something had come up, didn't you? What you *didn't* tell him was that the 'something' was your old bedmate!"

Jon's face went white in the bright glare of the electric light, and the scar on his forehead burned an angry, pulsing red. If she hadn't been beside herself already Jessica might have been wary of this grim-faced, unfamiliar Jon. But she was beyond that, beyond caring how he reacted to her outburst.

"And just what do you mean by that?" he asked softly—too softly. His eyes were flat mirrors of disenchantment, but Jessica was too furious, too overwrought to see.

"I mean I understand now why you've been treating me as if I were a vestal virgin these past few weeks," she shouted at him. "It's all falling into place, isn't it? You had Carol to take care of your—your physical needs, so you could leave me up on some chaste pedestal suitable for kid sisters and dingbats. You never really wanted me, Jon, did you? I was just something that happened to you because Carol wasn't around. Someone to amuse you, but not someone you really needed." She sat down suddenly on the sofa. "No wonder you wouldn't touch me. Why should you touch skinny little Jessica when you had glamorous, curvy Carol to keep you warm?''

If Jessica had been less intent on unloading her own anger she might have noticed the smoky glitter in Jon's eyes, seen the veins pounding in his neck as both fists clenched tight against his thighs. She might also have realized that, although every masculine inch of him was held tautly under control, he was very close to a rage that surpassed hers.

"So you want me to touch you, do you?" he said, in a voice that would have signaled danger if she'd been listening.

She lifted her eyebrows, and her nose turned up in a sneer. "What do *you* think?" she asked waspishly.

"I think," said Jon, with silken menace, "that if it's touching you want, Jessica, you're about to get it."

Jessica looked up then, and for the first time took in properly that she was not the only one who had lost her temper.

Jon's skin had gone unusually dark, and his eyes were no longer merely smoky—they were blazing.

"Wh-what...?" she began.

She got no further. In one stride he was beside her, towering over her. Then both his hands had gripped her elbows and he was pulling her onto her feet.

Jessica drew in her breath, startled out of her anger, as Jon's strong arms swept around her waist, crushing her roughly against him. She had just enough time to take in the punitive twist to his mouth before it descended over hers, not gently in the way she was used to, but fiercely, as if he wanted to hurt her. When he had kissed her before, he had given as much, or more than he'd taken. This time there was no giving—only a savage taking.

Jessica, tortured more by the pain in her heart than by what he was doing, struggled frantically to set herself free. But he only held her closer, forcing his tongue between her teeth—and then he began to lower her onto the floor.

Before she could take in what was happening he was lying on top of her, his breath coming in short, rasping gasps. One hand was on the neck of her nightgown, the other moving up her bare thigh.

Jessica twisted her head as his lips searched for her mouth, and, just for a second, as her eyes focused on the autumn shades of the carpet, she remembered another carpet she had lain on long ago—a carpet of green grass beside a lake. Jon's body had pressed her down on that day too, but then he had been laughing at first, and very quickly he had rolled off and moved away. This time there was no laughter, and although she pushed desperately at his shoulders he showed no signs whatever of moving away. Instead his hand was on her inner thigh, and the belt of her robe was undone. Once she might have welcomed this, welcomed him, pulled him even closer and helped him remove her scanty clothing. But not now. Not like this, when there was no affection or caring in the fingers that moved over her, but only an unrestrained desire to exact revenge.

His hand slid closer to its destination, to the place where it had never been before, and his body, pinning her down, became heavier, a trap from which she couldn't hope to escape.

"Damn you," she thought she heard him swear beneath his breath.

"Jon!" Emerging at last from the initial shock, and roused from her disbelieving immobility, Jessica began to struggle more wildly. "Jon, please. Don't..." Her cry was that of some soft furry thing in distress. Or that of a wounded child.

And Jon, who had seemed oblivious to everything but his own anger, heard it, and was suddenly still.

He lay there for a moment, not moving, not even breathing. Then very slowly he pushed himself onto his elbows, turned his face away, and stood up.

Jessica stared at the white ceiling, her eyes huge, violet and lambent, with tears just beginning to glitter against the lashes. As she began to tug listlessly at her rumpled clothes, Jon glanced down at her, then looked away again and turned his back.

With quiet desperation Jessica fastened the belt of her robe, picked herself off the floor and, wrapping both arms tightly around her chest, sank heavily onto the sofa.

Jon still stood with his back to her. It was completely rigid. His hands were rammed into his pockets, his legs a little apart, and his dark blond head bent forward between his shoulders. And even from the depths of her misery Jessica couldn't help thinking how breathtaking he looked from behind—as well as from every other angle.

For a long time there was silence in the room, a silence that was deep as a mountain cavern. Then, as if the words were wrenched from the innermost part of his being, Jon growled hoarsely and without even turning his head, "I'm sorry, Delaney."

Jessica, no longer angry, but gripped by a terrible desolation, stared at his formidable back and thought bleakly, That's it? You've just destroyed everything we might have had together and you're sorry! She put a finger to her lips, searching mindlessly for bruises. So he was sorry. And if that was all he had to say, then the only thing she could do was accept it, and get this agony over with at once. Because if he didn't leave soon she was afraid she would break down completely.

Her hand dropped to her lap. The only bruises she could find were on her heart. "So am I," she said quietly. "Please go now, Jon."

He turned then, and she saw that his face was very white and still, his eyes as gray and unreadable as rain.

"Delaney..." he muttered, stretching a hand toward her, and then letting it fall back against his side. "Delaney, I..."

She swallowed, her eyes wide with unshed tears. He was calling her Delaney again. But it was too late.

"*Go*, please, Jon," she whispered. "I—I don't want to see you again. Not ever."

When he didn't move she looked up and said decisively, "You must believe me."

Jon nodded, almost imperceptibly. His face was a carved, cold death mask, his gaze an unfathomable enigma.

"Yes," he said without emotion. "I must believe you." He turned away and began to make for the door as, automatically, Jessica hugged her robe around her, stood up, and started to follow him. When he reached the door she stopped suddenly and began to search behind her for support. Her groping fingers came in contact with the back of a chair and, holding it tightly, she maneuvered around it like a sleepwalker until she felt something solid press the back of her knees. Then she sank down to perch in precarious discomfort on the arm.

Jon was behind her, and she could still hear his breathing as she waited for the sound of his leaving. She knew he *would* leave, because there was nothing more to be said.

Feeling empty, drained and deathly cold, Jessica stared down at the pattern in the carpet, rust brown on beige with a hint of gold. And she knew that at any moment she would hear the door slam as Jon made his exit from her life.

But it didn't slam, and behind her there was no sound at all. When she could stand it no longer she lifted her head.

He was standing very still, looking at her. Even from a distance she could see the deep lines beside his mouth, the furrows between his shadowed eyes. He looked at her for a long time, almost as if he was storing away a memory. Then he took two quick strides back into the room, and when he was almost on top of her he raised his hand to her face.

Jessica flinched as she felt his firm fingers touch her cheek. Jon saw, and a spasm of something that might have been pain crossed his face. He dropped his arm abruptly. For a moment she thought he meant to speak, but instead he seemed to release his breath, and, growling words that sounded like, "Goodbye, Delaney. Be happy," he turned so swiftly that she scarcely realized he'd moved.

A door closed, and she was alone in the brightly lit room.

CHAPTER NINE

JESSICA stared over the top of her typewriter at a row of overflowing garbage cans in the lane behind her basement suite in East Vancouver. The paper in her machine was starkly blank.

It was the middle of January, a dull, drizzling, damp Vancouver day, but for a few gray moments the rain appeared to have stopped, and a stringy black cat had emerged from nowhere to rummage delicately through the rubbish. Jessica watched it idly, wondering if even that skinny scavenger found more promise in its life than she did.

It was a month now since she had given up her flat in Thunder Bay, after handing in her notice to Mr. Sanegra, who, to her surprise, seemed more relieved than upset to be losing her. It turned out that he had been waiting to give her job to his recently unemployed niece. Jessica was glad about that.

At first, in the days after that terrible scene in the early hours of an October morning, she had hoped, with a sort of desperate optimism, that somehow she would be able to pick up the pieces of herself and carry on. But when Halloween was over, and the golden leaves were reduced to shuffling brown heaps beneath bare-armed trees, she came to realize that too much had happened for her to be able to stay on in Thunder Bay.

Everywhere she went now her eyes filled with tears as she was confronted by places and people who reminded her of Jon. Not of Jon as she had last seen him, standing at the door of her parents' living room apologizing with grim austerity for his unforgivable behavior, but of the laughing, affectionate Jon she had grown to love.

Her parents came home from Europe in the middle of November, and Jessica discovered at last that her mother had known all along that no wedding had actually been planned. Nick had explained this to Meg Delaney the second time she'd phoned, after which all his mother's evasiveness had been directed to one end only—that of ensuring that her daughter would indeed marry Jon Stuart. If she hadn't been so mired in her own misery Jessica would have laughed at Meg's breezy assumption that pretending something would happen with sufficient dedication would inevitably make it come true. To this end, Nick had been sworn in as an accomplice.

"It ought to have worked," Meg had grumbled, casting a gloomy but still hopeful eye over the mountains of unnecessary presents.

"Ought it?" said Jessica vaguely, remembering that she had operated on much the same principle when she had begged Jon to be her fiancé. "Well, this time I'm afraid it didn't."

That was the point at which she had finally come to the conclusion that she couldn't stay much longer in Thunder Bay.

It was always dark when she drove to work on those cold, almost winter mornings, and she knew that when the snow came, as it would any day, it would mirror the icy blanket over her heart. Oh, she might get up, go to work, smile when she was smiled at, and pretend that nothing was wrong. But sooner or later it was inevitable that she would run into Jon. And with that certainty hanging overhead like a malevolent cloud she would never be able to continue writing and somehow go on to lead a contented and productive life in her home town.

Nor could she go back to being the carefree young woman who had so blithely asked Jon to be engaged to her. But surely somehow, somewhere, some time it would be possible to find...a kind of peace?

Perhaps far away in Vancouver things might be different. At home nothing would ever be the same again.

Jon hadn't attempted to see her after that fateful night, and on that score Jessica was surprised to find she felt relieved. When she had told him, in the first rush of grief and hurt, that she never wanted to see him again the words had been an emotional reflex to the unendurable shock of what he'd done—or almost done. Later, in the cold, calm light of rational thought, she understood that instinctively she had told him the simple truth.

She couldn't see Jon again. The pain would be too great to bear. Because Jon was no longer the friend she had known all her life, nor was he the man she had come to love and sometimes dreamed of having children with. Something had happened to that man, and the Jon of her dreams had disappeared forever when he'd lied to her and then turned into an avenging, aggressive stranger she didn't know. The man she loved no longer even existed. And the hollow ache, the loneliness, and the pain that tore permanently at her heart were desolate black voids which she occasionally thought would swallow her alive. In the end she knew her only hope was to get away, to a place where she could start life afresh.

Finally, with bitter resolution, she had booked her flight to Vancouver.

"But you can't leave before Christmas," Meg had protested.

"Oh, Mother, I'm sorry, but I have to." Jessica knew that however hard she might try to put on a cheerful front her presence could only cast a pall over her family's festivities.

Two weeks later she fled.

By the time her first green Christmas arrived she was installed in her basement suite which the advertisement had described as "compact and convenient." In fact it was cramped, dark and generally inconvenient. But it suited her mood. The tenants upstairs invited her to share their Christmas dinner, and, although they wouldn't let her refuse, as soon as she decently could she escaped from the jovial family atmosphere to return to the lonely privacy of her rooms.

In the evening her mother phoned.

"Jessica? Merry Christmas. Have you had a good day? I hope you haven't been moping." Meg's voice bristled with motherly suspicion.

"No, I've had a wonderful day," lied Jessica, falling back on her dramatic experience to convince her mother that all was right with her world. "I had dinner with the family upstairs."

"That's all right, then," said Meg, appeased. "Jessica——?"

"How was your Christmas?" asked Jessica quickly, before her mother could concoct further reasons to indulge in maternal anxiety.

"Well, I'm not sure," replied Meg airily. "Your dad's gone to bed complaining that his head keeps spinning around—but he assures us it has nothing at all to do with too much wine, Roger and Annette are shouting at each other over which one of them lost their plane tickets back to Toronto, and Nick's in the garage directing some *very* unsuitable language at a rusty water-pump bolt. At least, I *think* he said a rusty bolt, but it's hard to tell. Apart from that, everybody's fine. You should have come home, dear."

For the first time that Christmas Jessica actually felt like laughing. "Yes," she agreed weakly. "Yes, Mom, I guess I should."

"Mm. And dear..." Meg hesitated.

"Yes, Mom?"

"Jon's been around. He looks terrible. He was asking after you."

"Good," said Jessica, who didn't feel like laughing any more. She left her mother to guess whether she meant it was good that Jon looked terrible, or good that he had asked about her.

When she hung up the phone, once again she felt exposed and bleeding, as if the fragile defenses she had pulled around her like a protective skin had just been peeled off her layer by layer. And she knew she had to do something to keep her mind from straying back to Jon—who looked terrible and had been asking about her...

Swallowing hard, she crossed the room to glare with morose concentration at her typewriter. Eventually she unwrapped a fresh supply of paper, thumped herself down, and, with an inspiration that seemed to be ripped from her soul, finished the last two chapters of her book—which in the process changed from a light-hearted if somewhat bloody romp to a macabre psychological tragedy of love and death.

And that was Christmas.

Three weeks later, with the book consigned to the dark drawer where it belonged, Jessica was once again in front of her typewriter, watching the black cat slink off down the lane. She had given up the idea of writing the Great Canadian Mystery, having come to the reluctant conclusion that her talents didn't lie in a literary direction. Soon she would look for another office job, and in the autumn she could take up teaching again. Meanwhile, if she could only think of something to say it was time she wrote a bright and optimistic letter to her parents.

Optimism didn't come easily. She stared at the paper, and all it did was stare back, white and uninspiring. Then gradually, as her eyes misted over, Jon's face seemed to appear on it, gray and almost haggard, and in her mind she saw him pass a hand wearily over his eyes.

She shook her head, but the picture wouldn't go away. Strange. In all the weeks since she had seen him she hadn't given a lot of thought to Jon's feelings. She hadn't wanted to. Vaguely she'd supposed he was back with Carol, and not feeling much at all. Even though it could make no difference to her anymore, the thought turned like a knife in her stomach.

On the surface, of course, there was no mystery about Jon's attitude. She forced herself to face the facts. He had just been amusing himself with her while Carol was gone. And later he'd been arrogantly enraged over the spilled wine. When she'd goaded him he had lost his temper completely, and behaved ... Jessica squeezed her eyes shut, not wanting to remember how he'd behaved. Then he'd growled an apology before going nonchalantly back to Carol. Only... Jessica pulled moodily at a lock of her hair. Only, that wasn't altogether like Jon, was it? But then none of it had been like the Jon she loved, so perhaps she had never really known him, after all.

She sighed. What did it matter? Jon was part of another life. A life that was over and done with. Lifting her hands reluctantly, she began to type.

"Dear Mother and Dad: there's a black cat..."

The next word was a blur of jumbled typescript as the doorbell rang shrilly and Jessica's fingers jumped all over the keyboard.

No one ever called this late in the afternoon. It must be a salesman. Muttering under her breath, she stumbled to her feet and crossed to the narrow front door. It stuck as usual, but when she finally yanked it open it wasn't a salesman who stood there.

It was Jon.

Jessica gasped. She must be suffering from hallucinations. First Jon's face on her paper—and now this. She closed her eyes.

When she opened them again he was still there.

Slowly, incredulously her eyes traveled over him. He was wearing a dark suit, and he looked older and more unapproachable than she remembered. His face wasn't clear in the twilight, but she could see his mouth, sensual as ever, but pulled into a bleak, straight line. She could see his scar, too. It looked more like an open wound now than a faded memento of a youthful recklessness.

Jessica stared for a long time, as he stared back at her without speaking.

Then, very quietly, she shut the door in his face.

Seconds later she stood with her forehead pressed against the painted wood, waiting for the sound of his footsteps going away. But there was no sound, and in the end she could stand it no longer.

Thin yellow curtains covered a small window beside the door, and she put her eye to the point where they didn't quite meet.

Jon was still there, his fist raised to knock, and suddenly the streetlights came on.

He stood there for some time, with his fist a few inches from the door. Then, as if he were lowering a heavy weight, he let his arm drop to his side.

Jessica's mouth opened to say something she knew he wouldn't hear, but at the same moment he swung around with startling abruptness, and, as she watched, mesmerized, he walked quickly away into the dusk.

But just before he turned she saw his eyes.

CHAPTER TEN

JESSICA stood in front of the window watching the persistent black cat. Black cats were supposed to be lucky, she remembered—and apparently this one was. It had just swallowed a chicken bone with no visible ill effect. Was that supposed to be an omen? She shrugged. If it was, she didn't believe it.

Only ten minutes had passed since Jon had walked away from her door, but those minutes had seemed like ten years. She had been so sure, so very sure that she didn't want to see him again. And when she had seen him, her heart hadn't started to sing. It had dropped like frozen lead to her knees. So she had shut the door.

But afterward...afterward she had seen his eyes. And she couldn't forget them. They had been cavernous, darker than midnight in the evening light, and filled with such bleak desolation, such fathomless emptiness that something hard and cold inside her had begun to melt. She had never seen eyes look like that. Except, perhaps, her own sometimes lately, when she had foolishly looked in the mirror...

Slowly, moving like an automaton, she walked over to her cupboard to fetch a coat.

Where would Jon go in this neighborhood if he had nowhere he had to be, nothing to do, and a desperate need to blot out the world? Well, he certainly wouldn't throw himself into the ocean, she reflected. Not Jon. And he didn't seem to have a car with him...

167

There was a pub near the bus stop. It was a nice pub, warm, intimate and inviting. As she had not been. It was the only hope.

Clutching her coat against the rain, Jessica hurried down the two short blocks to the bus stop. Jon wasn't there, but the lights of the pub winked a welcome. Hesitantly, afraid of what she wouldn't see, Jessica pushed open the heavy door.

He was there, but he had his back to her, at a small table in a darkened corner. His coat was slung carelessly over a chair, and she could see that he had loosened his tie. His broad shoulders were hunched, his head bent forward. And in the midst of her own unhappiness Jessica's heart constricted. She watched for a moment as he lifted a glass and took a long swig of what looked like a double whiskey. Then she made her way steadily around the tables to stand in front of him.

He didn't look up.

"Jon," she said. "It's me."

He did look up then, and she choked back a gasp at what she saw. His face was hard, devoid of any emotion except a kind of harsh regret. His eyes were hard too now, and yet empty, circled with lines of fatigue. And behind the emptiness was an almost unbearable pain. As she stared at him, her emotions in such tattered confusion that she had to grab a chair for support, his heavy brows drew together in a scowl that looked as if it had been there forever. There was no vestige left in that harsh, set visage of the boy, and later the man, who had laughed with her and teased her down the years.

Now he was staring at her, his bronzed skin darker than usual, and when he spoke even his voice was different.

"What have you come for, Delaney? To see if your revenge has been complete?" He shrugged, and then added bitterly, "I suppose I owe you that much."

Jessica shook her head dumbly. "No, Jon, of course not. I don't want revenge. I've come because—because..." She saw his head snap up, and his gray eyes darken with suspicion—and something else. "I've come because I love you."

And it was true. She knew that beyond all doubt. Whatever Jon had done she would always love him. She might not be able to make a life with him. But she loved him. She couldn't help it.

He didn't react at first, and when he did it was almost in slow motion, as he lowered the glass, placed both hands flat on the table, and pushed himself on to his feet.

"Do you mean that?" he asked, his eyes not moving from her face.

Jessica nodded, unable to speak.

Jon didn't speak either. Instead he moved around the table with a speed which she had not thought possible, and took her into his arms. And as his lips claimed hers, deeply and warmly and with a remembered sweetness, behind them a ripple of approving laughter swept the room.

Jon lifted his head. "Let's get out of here," he said, grabbing her arm and slinging his jacket over his shoulder.

Jessica stumbled after him as he started to tow her across the floor, but her hip caught the edge of the table, shaking it, and Jon's glass teetered crazily. Then it tumbled over and shot its contents in a long brown stream all over the back of his legs.

Jon stopped in his tracks and swung swiftly around to face her. "What on earth...?" His shout echoed across the room, and Jessica gazed up at him, horrified. "Good grief," he muttered, lowering his voice with an obvious effort. "Is it your mission in life to marinade me in my own booze, Delaney? Because if it is..." He paused, and brushed an arm across his forehead as Jessica backed warily away. "No, of course it isn't," he amended. "Come on."

"Wait," cried Jessica. "I must help to clean up this mess." She smiled apologetically at a disgruntled-looking waiter who was advancing with a bucket and mop.

"Forget it," snapped the waiter. "You get out of here, miss, before the pair of you do any more damage."

Jessica took one look at his face and decided not to argue—especially as Jon was now behind her and had seized both her elbows to hustle her ahead of him through the door.

Once outside, he turned her to face him, ignoring the rain that was now pelting down in black sheets, and took her face in his hands. Even in the dim winter lighting she could see the doubt in his eyes, the grim expectation of rejection. But when she only smiled, he gave a low groan and bent his head to kiss her with a slow, aching tenderness that told her, as nothing else could have done, that by some miracle the Jon she loved had come back. And she knew that in spite of all the anguish of past months there was a chance—perhaps only a slim one— that everything might somehow be all right.

He took his time kissing her, and she kissed him back, neither of them caring about the rain, with the result that by the time they had dripped their way to her front door some fifteen minutes later Jon was soaked through to the skin. Jessica, who was wearing a coat, was reasonably dry.

"You'd better take your clothes off," she said briskly, taking great care not to look at him. "You'll find plenty of towels in the bathroom."

"Do you know," said Jon, his voice holding a hint of grim humor, "those are about the most promising words I've heard in months?"

"Oh, just get on with it," snapped Jessica, giving him a shove in the direction of the bathroom, and not sure whether she wanted to laugh or cry. At the moment she wasn't sure of anything.

Jon got on with it, and in a few minutes, as she stood in the middle of the living room toweling her hair with a tea cloth, he was back, wearing only a thick white bath towel around his waist.

Jessica moistened her lips. His glistening male torso, poised like that of Adonis restored to her briefly by the gods, was enough to rob her of speech. His casual magnetism took her breath away, and she found it hard to believe that less than an hour ago she had never expected to see this man again. An hour ago she hadn't wanted to see him, either, but now...

Now she didn't know if she was standing on her head or her heels, because although his eyes still reflected a sort of defensive hardness there was a crooked warmth to his mouth, and when he had kissed her...

"Jon," she said quietly, "why did you come?"

He took a step forward, and placed both hands lightly on her shoulders. "I asked you a similar question a while back. My answer's the same as yours."

Her eyes widened. "Because—because you love me?"

"Yes, Delaney." His eyes were almost stern on her face. "Heaven help me, and in spite of what you must think, I've never loved anyone else."

"Oh, Jon!" She didn't know what had happened, why hope that had been extinguished forever was rising like the phoenix from its ashes. But it didn't matter. With a sigh of exhausted joy she wrapped her arms around his neck and rested her cheek on his naked chest. "Neither have I. Only at first I was too stupid to see it."

"Not stupid," said Jon, stroking her damp hair. "Just a dingbat. I was the one who was stupid. Criminally stupid. Can you forgive me?"

Jessica looked up into his face, saw the shadows that still haunted his eyes, and knew that whatever had happened between them that October night was in the past.

"Yes," she said quietly, tightening her grip on his neck. "I can forgive you. We'll have to forgive each other. Won't we?"

Jon shook his head. "I have nothing to forgive you for, Delaney."

Her lips parted in the ghost of a smile. "Not even for—what was it you said? Marinading you in your own booze?"

"Ah." Jon laughed ruefully, and kissed the top of her head. "That's a very bad habit, I grant you. One I shall have to cure you of quite swiftly."

"How?" asked Jessica curiously.

"Like this." Jon unclasped her arms suddenly, scooped her over his shoulder, crossed the room in one stride, and dumped her down on the blue sofa. Then he sat down beside her, cupped his hands on her cheeks, and kissed her very thoroughly on the mouth.

But when he had finished he moved away from her to lean back with one arm resting along the back of the sofa. "We have to talk, Delaney," he said quietly.

She nodded, a little stab of fear clutching her heart. As long as they could speak to each other with their bodies, she knew there would be no problems between them. But when it came to emotions beyond mere physical hunger...that was where they seemed to come apart.

"Yes," she agreed glumly. "Yes, you're right. We must. But..." She shivered. "I'm almost afraid to talk, Jon."

"I don't blame you. Not after the way I behaved when we last met." He wasn't looking at her now, and his voice was flat.

She stared at the taut bronzed skin across his chest. "But you wouldn't have done that, would you?" she said with sudden certainty. "If I hadn't goaded you beyond endurance," she added. "And even then you wouldn't have—wouldn't have..."

"Forced you?" he said harshly. "Or were you going to use a much more loaded word? No. You're right. I wouldn't have. But I had no business going as far as I did. I was in a rage and I wanted to punish you." He paused, and she saw his fists clench convulsively. "It wasn't just the spilled wine, it was... Delaney, have you any idea what it was like those weeks when we were together? Seeing you almost every day, nearly crazy with wanting you, and knowing you were mine for the taking? And at the same time never able to forget that you were Delaney, Roger's sister, and that if I so much as touched you I was likely to light a fire I couldn't put out? I couldn't contemplate that. I'd spent too many years trying to look after you, I suppose, and the thought that I could be the one to..."

"Deflower me?" suggested Jessica wryly.

He grimaced. "Mm. I couldn't do it. And then, when I was already mad, you started taunting me about not touching you, about—what did you call her? Glamorous, curvy Carol? Well, at that moment something snapped. It wasn't Carol I wanted, it was you. And you were almost daring me to take you." He ran a hand over his eyes, and shook his head as if trying to banish a nightmare. Then he said bleakly, "It was too much, Delaney. Like I said, something snapped. But that's not an excuse. Because there isn't any excuse for what I did."

"Perhaps not," agreed Jessica slowly. "At least, there wouldn't have been if you'd actually done it. But you didn't. You wouldn't." She hesitated. "Jon, *why* were you so angry? Why didn't you explain? About Carol, I mean. There was an explanation, wasn't there?"

He nodded, his eyes fixed grimly above her head. "Of course. And part of the reason I didn't explain was because I was just too blazing mad. The other part was that I didn't see why I should have to."

Jessica blinked. "But you *must* have seen how it looked to me—after you'd canceled our date..."

He frowned. "Yes. Looking back, perhaps I do see. At the time all I knew was that I was having a quiet meal with an old friend who needed help, when I was assaulted by an enraged dingbat on the rampage with my own wine. And by the time I'd taken Carol home, cleaned myself up, thought about all the unmentionable things I'd like to do to you, believe me, I was in no mood for explanations."

"Well, yes, I do see that," said Jessica. "But I still don't understand why you didn't understand how I felt."

Jon pushed a hand through his hair, leaving it carelessly disheveled. "Delaney, I asked you to join us. Did I *look* like a man who had anything he wanted to hide?"

She hadn't thought of that. "No, I suppose not," she agreed reluctantly. "Not when you put it like that."

"Precisely."

"But, Jon..." She struggled for words to make him grasp what she meant. "Don't you see? You *lied* to me. Of course I was upset, and when I saw you with Carol I stopped thinking straight for a moment."

"Mm," he acknowledged, his full lips curving wryly. "I suppose I should have remembered that my dingbat's thought processes don't always progress in a straight line."

"That's not fair," said Jessica calmly, not minding being patronized for once because she sensed that he was only teasing, and that the banter was his way of holding off some unbearably heavy burden. "After all, you *were* having dinner with Carol, and all you told Nick was that 'something' had come up."

"I know," he conceded. "And of course if *you* had answered the phone I would have explained—as I intended to the next day in any case. But I was damned if I was discussing my business with young Nick." He leaned forward suddenly and caught her wrist. "My dear, there's been nothing between Carol and me for a long time. But we're still friends, and when she phoned to say she was in trouble, and asked me to meet her...what could I say?"

"No?" suggested Jessica.

"Delaney, that's not like you. When have you ever let down a friend who needed your help?"

She shifted uncomfortably. "I haven't. All right, what sort of trouble?"

"Financial. Creditors getting insistent and threatening to repossess her car and various other items she considers essential. Carol's always had champagne tastes. She wanted to borrow money, that's all, and I suppose of all her acquaintances I seemed the most likely pigeon."

"So you lent it to her," said Jessica, knowing with certainty that he had, although she would never have made the mistake of taking him for a pigeon.

"Yes, I did. After I'd bought her dinner and had my own wine dumped over me by the woman I was just beginning to realize I was in love with. It wasn't one of my better evenings, let me tell you—and I didn't lend her as much as she'd hoped for. Just enough to get her straightened around." He smiled cynically. "Incidentally, she's already paid it back. New job and new boyfriend, I believe."

Yes, that sounded like Jon. Helpful, but not a pushover, and unlikely to approve of people who got into debt.

"I should have trusted you," she stated, watching his thumb as it traced a thoughtful pattern across her palm.

He lifted his head, and she saw that his eyes were empty again, turned inward on some private hell.

"Yes," he said, in an odd, gravelly voice. "You should have trusted me then. It would have saved us both a lot of grief. But afterward—how could you?" He dropped her hand suddenly and stood up, a magnificent figure with his long naked limbs, and the white towel accentuating the smooth tanned gold of his skin. "Delaney," he said, staring grimly down at her, "I tried to apologize that night, but when I realized what I'd done, what you must be thinking . . ."

"But you hadn't really done anything," she whispered. "I see that now. And you wouldn't have."

"No. But how could I expect you to believe that? I've never behaved like that to any woman—and when I did . . ." His jaw tightened, and he turned away, then forced himself to look at her again. "When I did—it was to you. Of all people. And if I couldn't forgive myself, Delaney, why in the world should you?" His voice was raw, filled with self-recrimination. "You said you didn't want to see me again—and I couldn't expect you to feel otherwise. I thought the only thing I could do then was respect your wishes, and stay out of your life."

"Oh, Jon." Jessica stretched both hands up to him, and with a low groan he caught them and dropped on to the sofa beside her. "Jon, I lost my temper too—before you did. And afterward I thought you weren't the same person, weren't the Jon I loved any longer. But I should have known. And even before that I—I should have known right from the beginning that I loved you. *That's* why I chose you to be engaged to."

He smiled and put his hand absently on her thigh, the tortured look fading a little. "And that's why I agreed to do it, I suspect. Because I loved you too, Delaney."

He held one small palm against his chest, and Jessica placed the other one beside it.

"Is that why you let your mother believe we were getting married?" she asked with sudden illumination.

"Probably." He grinned crookedly.

"Disgraceful," murmured Jessica, trailing her fingers languidly across his chest. Immediately he bent down to kiss her, and the taste of his warm lips and the sweet, spicy smell of his breath were more intoxicating than any wine she had ever drunk.

Then her fingers moved down to his waist, discovered the loosely wrapped towel, and began to explore further.

At once Jon caught her wrist, took her by both elbows, held her away and said firmly, "No. We haven't finished our discussion, Delaney."

Jessica didn't want to discuss, she wanted to continue her delicious explorations, to feel Jon's smooth male skin beneath her lips. But he wouldn't let her.

"No," he repeated flatly, as she reached again for his waist. "No. We've made too many mistakes already, and if I let you do that we both know where it will end."

"But that's where I want it to end," protested Jessica.

"I know," he growled. "Lord knows, so do I. But not yet. Not until I'm sure..."

Jessica pulled away from him. "Sure that I've grown up?" she demanded, eyes accusing.

"No. Sure that you know what you're doing, sure that you can trust me after——"

"I know exactly what I'm doing," interrupted Jessica, her shoulders sagging limply with relief. "And of course I trust you." She smiled mischievously. "Provided that you trust me. You never know, I might decide you taste best pickled in wine..."

"Oh, might you?" he said. "Well, for your information I've had about enough of your alcoholic antics. And if you try it again you're likely to find yourself viewing the world from a very undignified angle." He reached for her with a retaliatory gleam in his eye.

Jessica laughed and jumped up, but he caught her at once, pulled her onto his knee and kissed her with exquisite expertise. She was just beginning to melt into liquid jelly against his skin when he released her with devastating briskness, and said quite matter-of-factly, "Have you eaten today?"

"You're talking about food?" she exclaimed disbelievingly. "Now?" And then, when she realized the pangs in her stomach were not all caused by Jon's appetite-arousing closeness, she added on a note of surprise, "No. I guess I haven't."

"I thought not. Bacon and eggs, then," he stated authoritatively, tipping her off his knee and depositing her onto the sofa. "I suppose you do have food in that cubby-hole of a kitchen?"

"Of course," said Jessica indignantly.

"Good. Wait here, then. I won't be long."

Jessica did as she was told, mainly because she was too dazed by the events of the past hour to do anything else. She couldn't believe that her life, which only this morning had seemed so unrelentingly black, should so quickly have turned to a wonderful, rosy pink.

A few minutes later Jon called her to the kitchen.

"Sit," he ordered, waving her to her own chair.

Jessica sat, not even bothering to object that she wasn't a dog, as Jon thumped two heaped plates of bacon and eggs on the table and sat down opposite her.

He was still wearing only a towel, which made it very hard to concentrate on eggs.

"What made you decide to come all the way out here?" she asked, almost shyly. "I mean, are you on business as well as——?"

"Pleasure?" he asked, raising a deliciously suggestive eyebrow.

"Er—yes."

"No." His expression sobered immediately. "I came to find you, Delaney. I've been going through seven kinds of self-inflicted hell these past weeks..."

"So have I," whispered Jessica.

He shut his eyes briefly. "I know. I'm sorry. But, you see, in my case it got so bad that Brad started to complain I was scaring away the clients. And in the end I couldn't take it any longer. I knew you'd left town, of course, but I had to find out if you were...all right. So I went to see your family on Christmas Day. Your mother, who seemed quite put out with me, said you were fine. But Nick pulled me aside and told me you weren't fine. He said you'd resembled a love-sick noodle the day you left——"

"Thanks, Nick," muttered Jessica.

"And that when he'd talked to you on the phone you'd sounded like his car on a rainy day."

"That bad?" she exclaimed.

"Apparently. He also said it was all my fault, and would I please come out here and tell you to snap out of it, because your mother's going crazy with worry."

"Oh," said Jessica in a small voice. "Oh, dear."

"Yes, that's what I thought. Also, I was going crazy without you." He made a face. "I've been going crazy without you for years, only I wouldn't accept it. Anyway, I took Nick at his word. As soon as I could get away, I came."

"And I shut the door on you," said Jessica, with a break in her voice.

"Yes." For a moment his face looked as it had when she'd seen it through the gap in the curtains. "And how could I blame you? I did think about breaking it down, but in the end I decided I didn't have that right."

"I saw you," murmured Jessica softly. "Oh, Jon, you looked so—so..." Her eyes filled with tears. "So terribly alone. And I couldn't bear it..."

"You have a kind and generous heart, Delaney," he said gruffly. "That's why I love you."

"Oh, Jon." All at once the emotions of the day became too much for Jessica and, food forgotten, she flew around the table to fling her arms about his neck. "Oh, Jon, I love you too."

"Hey, watch it!" He laughed as his chair teetered precariously and then collapsed beneath the onslaught. "I believe it's usual to celebrate these things with champagne, love, not broken ribs." He wound a lock of her hair around his fingers, and pulled it, very gently.

"No champagne for you," declared Jessica, sitting firmly on his stomach as he lay on the floor smiling up at her. "You've had quite enough to drink already." She ran a finger deliberately down his bare chest to his navel.

"All right," he agreed, gasping. "No champagne. Now get your beautiful body off my digestive system before I'm forced to do something drastic."

"Like what?" asked Jessica hopefully.

"Like changing the menu to bed instead of late breakfast," he threatened, catching her finger before it could explore any lower.

"Mm. I think I'd like that."

"I dare say you would, but *not* until we've finished our discussion. Now get off before I throw you off."

She saw that in spite of the teasing note he meant business.

"My eggs are cold," she grumbled, as she returned without enthusiasm to the table.

"Serves you right," responded Jon unsympathetically. "Eat them anyway."

Jessica discovered she was by now so hungry that it was easier to do as he said than argue.

When the last mouthful of egg had disappeared she looked at him across the table and asked a little grumpily, "What do you want to talk about, then?"

"Us. You've said you can trust me, but can you get it into your beautiful head and keep it there that I'm not 'good old Jon' any longer? That I'm a man, Delaney? A man who loves you?" His eyes were smokier than ever in the bright glare of the kitchen light.

"Of course," said Jessica, serious now. "I've been very well aware that you're—a man for a long time now. Ever since that night you pretended to be my fiancé. Only—only it was so hard to get used to the idea, and I couldn't believe it had really happened."

Jon nodded. "I know. I felt the same." He picked up a knife and ran it absently between his fingers. "Perhaps when it came right down to it the problem wasn't you at all. It was my inability to get past the fact that you were funny, maddening little Delaney. How could I even *think* of making love to Roger's sister? You may have been twenty-six years old, but to me you were still a beautiful child." He hesitated. "Do you remember a day about four years ago, down by Boulevard Lake...?"

"Yes," said Jessica, smiling reminiscently. "You fell on top of me, and I laughed at you, and you got mad..."

"For obvious reasons."

"They weren't all that obvious at the time."

"They were to me. I knew I had to forget what had happened, and make sure it didn't happen again."

"Hence Carol and Heather and all the others," remarked Jessica dryly.

"Not so many others. And they didn't last. Who's Heather?" he added, looking startled.

"The girl at Brenda's party."

"Oh, that Heather. I never went out with her. She was a friend's girlfriend."

"You might have said so."

"Why? I thought the uncertainty would do you good." Jon grinned unrepentantly.

Jessica glared at him. "Let's get back to that afternoon by the lake," she said severely.

He nodded, amusement falling away like summer mist. "All right. The fact is, I succeeded in convincing myself I'd forgotten that afternoon quite nicely. Until the day you asked me to get engaged."

"I started something, didn't I?" she agreed.

"Indeed you did. In fact, you were asking for trouble as usual. Which you're about to get."

He rose abruptly, swooped around the table, and, as she gaped up at him, picked her up out of her chair and carried her back to the sofa.

"Is this trouble?" she asked happily, as he settled her in the crook of his arm.

"It will be. I'm working up to it."

Suddenly, and quite inexplicably, Jessica started to cry.

"Hey!" exclaimed Jon, staring down at her in bewilderment. "Delaney, what's the matter? What have I done now? I was joking, for heaven's sake."

"I know," she sniffed. "It's just that I'm so—so happy."

Jon raised his eyes to the light bulb. "Oh, well, if *that's* all," he muttered, pulling out a handkerchief to wipe her face. "I bet you cry at weddings too, don't you?"

She nodded. "I'm afraid I do."

"Even your own?"

"Oh, no." She smiled dreamily. "I'm sure I won't cry at my own. I'll be *too* happy. At least . . ." She stopped, disconcerted to remember that Jon had not actually asked her to marry him.

"At least, what?"

"At least, I won't cry if I'm marrying the right man," she finished hopefully. When he didn't answer, she looked up at him with an indignant scowl. "Jon Stuart, are you trying to make me propose to you?"

"Yes," admitted Jon smugly. "That's the price you'll have to pay for being a thoroughly flaky dingbat—who may not be at all suited to partner a sober accountant."

"Idiot," scoffed Jessica, biting her lip to keep from laughing. "All right." Suddenly she wriggled out from under his arm to kneel down in front of him, clasping her hands to her breast. "Will you marry me, Jon Stuart?" she asked demurely. "And make me the happiest woman in the world?"

"Just try and stop me." Jon reached down to pull her roughly onto his knee.

"What am I going to do with you, Delaney?" he groaned, burying his face in her hair.

"I could make a suggestion," she replied, folding her hands primly in her lap.

"Oh, you could, could you?" he murmured, as her soft curls brushed across his face. "So could I."

Catching her wrists, he pushed her back against the cushions, pinning her arms at her sides and bending over her so that she couldn't move. Not that she wanted to move, because his mouth was claiming hers, and his hands were under her sweater, teasing her breasts. Gently he eased a long leg between her thighs as one hand moved to the fastening of her jeans to ease down the zip. Then his fingers were sliding over the silky smoothness of her hips, stroking her thighs...

Jessica gave a little murmur of delight, slipping her hands behind his back, feeling the tough resilience of his skin, and curving her body into his, wanting more, much more, wanting all of him...

"Jon," she whispered urgently against his cheek. "Please, Jon..."

"Blast!" To Jessica's stunned consternation, the moment she spoke Jon wrenched himself away from her

and sat up. After that he began to swear, quietly and
proficiently, and for quite some time.

"Jon, what's the matter?" she cried, anxious and
bereft and with the blood still pounding painfully in her
veins.

"I can't do it," he groaned.

"Can't do what?" Now she was thoroughly alarmed.

"I can't take you to bed this instant and make
passionate love to you all night."

"Why not?" Jessica frowned, not seeing the problem.

He groaned again. "Because you're Delaney. I've
spent too many years attempting to protect you from
people like me. We've got to get married, love. Prefer-
ably tomorrow. Or do you suppose we can find a justice
of the peace to marry us now?" He pulled her jeans
quickly up over her hips, and stood up.

"No," said Jessica gazing up at him, and resigning
herself to the inevitable. "But you can get a special li-
cense, and Father Michael can marry us in Thunder Bay
in a couple of weeks. He's a family friend, and I'm sure
he'll fit us in." She sighed. "It seems awfully far away,
doesn't it? But it'll take time for me to get things settled
here. Oh, Jon." She smiled up at him ruefully. "I'm so
glad to be going home again. I wish it could be
tomorrow..."

Jon pushed his hands into his pockets, and turned
away. "So do I," he said with rough tenderness. "But
we'll manage. And I swear I'll make it worth the wait."

Jessica had never had any doubt whatever that he
would.

It was cold and bright on the February afternoon when
Jon and Jessica were married, and the scent of fresh
snow was in the air. There was ice on the lake now, and
the bare trees bore no traces of their colorful autumn
splendor.

Because the wedding had been arranged in what Morag and Meg referred to as unnecessary haste, the question of holding it in a church had scarcely come up, especially after Ben and Brenda had offered their lakeside home for the quiet ceremony preferred by both bride and groom—and acceded to with glum resignation by their mothers.

Now, after what had seemed an endless two weeks to both Jessica and Jon, the latter stood beside Roger—who had flown in for the wedding—in the beautiful, high-ceilinged room overlooking the water. He glanced at his watch. Two minutes to go. Surely even the dingbat wasn't going to be late for her wedding? Unpunctuality had never been one of her faults. In fact, more often than not she was early.

The small company of assembled guests began to shuffle impatiently. Then, just as Jon was about to murmur something unprintable to Roger, he heard a familiar mechanical roaring sound in the distance. It was not a sound calculated to ease his mind. Everyone else heard it at the same moment, and lifted their heads in bemused astonishment.

"She wouldn't," muttered Jon out of the corner of his mouth. "She said she intended to make an entrance, but surely even Delaney——" He broke off as a flash of outrageous orange burst through the trees, backfired, and roared to a stop just inches from the edge of the lake.

"She wouldn't," Jon repeated, as Jessica's father, looking pained, and Nick, looking unnaturally spruce in a suit, stepped out of the Orange Peril and turned to assist the bride and a very pregnant Brenda, who was to be her bridesmaid. Jon was just heaving a sigh of exasperated relief when from across the room he heard Meg Delaney moan something which sounded like, "Oh, no! We ordered a *limousine*."

He closed his eyes, then turned to Roger and said gloomily, "I take it back. She would."

A moment later Jessica, dressed in pale mauve silk, floated serenely through the door and came toward him.

"*Why* the Peril?" he demanded under his breath, when she stood beside him. "Trusting yourself to that aging muscle car—today of all days..."

"The limousine broke down. The Peril seemed the next best thing." She smiled up at him so beguilingly, and looked so incredibly lovely, that he lowered his head so that the whole world wouldn't see the naked love and passion in his eyes.

"Oh, Delaney," he groaned, stifling a sudden urge to laugh. "Delaney, to anyone else your own car or your father's would have seemed the next best thing. Didn't it occur to you...?" He stopped, because his mother was glaring at him reprovingly, the guests had stopped shuffling and were waiting in expectant silence, and Father Michael was clearing his throat.

He smiled down at his bride, took her hand, and waited solemnly for the words which would join him forever to the woman with whom he would spend the rest of his life.

"I, Jon," said Father Michael.

"I, Jon," he repeated gravely.

"Take you, Jessica..."

As Father Michael's eyebrows rose up to meet his hairline, Jon, eyes brimming with irrepressible laughter, bent down to murmur in Jessica's ear, "I, Jon, take you, Delaney..."

And Jessica, eyes brimming with love as well as laughter, lifted her face to his and whispered, "I take you, too."

"Harrumph!" Father Michael cleared his throat again, noisily. Sobering, the guilty pair turned back to face him—and a few minutes later Jon Stuart and Jessica

Delaney became man and wife, with all the solemnity that befitted a dignified occasion.

"I'd better make the most of it, hadn't I?" Jon said to Jessica when, with guests clamoring all around them, he managed to get her to himself in a corner.

"Most of what?" she asked.

"The solemnity of the occasion," he replied, pulling a very long face.

"Why?" she asked suspiciously.

"Because," he said, unable to control the grin that split his features, "I have a feeling that from now on suitable solemnity may play a disgracefully small part in life with my Delaney."

Her eyes laughed back at him. "And you should always trust your instincts," she agreed.

As Jon's instincts at that moment told him to take her in his arms, kiss her soundly, and make love to her on the spot, it was just as well that Morag came bustling up to them to tell them it was time to cut the cake.

**Harlequin is proud to present our
best authors and their best books.
Always the best for your reading
pleasure!**

Throughout 1993, Harlequin will bring you
exciting books by some of the top names in
contemporary romance!

In June,
look for
*Threats and
Promises* by

The plan was to make her nervous. . . .

Lauren Stevens was so preoccupied with her new looks
and her new business that she really didn't notice a
pattern to the peculiar ''little incidents''—incidents
that could eventually take her life. However, she did
notice the sudden appearance of the attractive and
interesting Matt Kruger who *claimed* to be a close
friend of her dead brother. . . .

**Find out more in THREATS AND
PROMISES . . . available wherever Harlequin
books are sold.**

BOB2

New York Times Bestselling Author

Sandra Brown

Tomorrow's Promise

**She cherished the memory
of love but was consumed
by a new passion too
fierce to ignore.**

For Keely Preston, the memory of her husband
Mark has been frozen in time since the day he was
listed as missing in action. And now, twelve years
later, twenty-six men listed as MIA have been
found.

Keely's torn between hope for Mark and despair
for herself. Because now, after all the years of
waiting, she has met another man!

**Don't miss TOMORROW'S PROMISE by
SANDRA BROWN.**

**Available in June wherever Harlequin
books are sold.**

TP

HARLEQUIN ◆ PRESENTS®

A Year
DOWN UNDER

In 1993, Harlequin Presents celebrates the land down
under. In June, let us take you to the Australian Outback,
in OUTBACK MAN by Miranda Lee,
Harlequin Presents #1562.

Surviving a plane crash in the Australian Outback is
surely enough trauma to endure. So why does Adrianna
have to be rescued by Bryce McLean, a man so gorgeous
that he turns all her cherished beliefs upside-down? But
the desert proves to be an intimate and seductive setting
and suddenly Adrianna's only realities are the red-hot
dust *and* Bryce....

Share the adventure—and the romance—
of A Year Down Under!

Available this month in
A YEAR DOWN UNDER

SECRET ADMIRER
by Susan Napier
Harlequin Presents #1554
Wherever Harlequin books are sold.

YDU-MY